Critical acclaim for the books in
THE RUNNING TIDE series.

'For those who like good, old-fashioned tales of courage and adventure . . . the hardships of the voyage, the terrible beauty of the ocean and the scenery are compellingly described'
Observer

'Written in the spirit of the traditional adventure story . . . offers readers not just a breath but a gale of fresh air'
Independent

'Epic . . . of colossal scope . . . bursting with life, hopes and discovery' *Scotsman*

'Beautifully written . . . ideal for long, dark winter nights with a warm fire to sit beside, for even in the twenty-something degree heat of summer the blizzards made me shiver'
Bookseller

'An adventure . . . with the salty tang of life at sea, the drama and mixed emotions of the whale hunt, and the harshness of the far North' *Times Educational Supplement*

'Any child who loves ships will feel the wind and salt spray'
Mail on Sunday

'His prose is evocative and atmospheric, capturing the sound and taste of the   a surprise ending' *Times E*

STEPHEN POTTS

Stephen wanted to be a doctor from an early age. He studied hard, spending his spare time on the water, or with his head in a book. He has always read hungrily, from Cornflakes packets to Tolstoy, but didn't think about writing until medical school at Oxford. Initially he wrote as a distraction from exams, and subsequently as a relief from punishing hours as a junior doctor. The longer he's spent in medicine – he's now a consultant in an Edinburgh teaching hospital – the more seriously he's taken his writing. When he's not working on his next book, he's on his boat, together with his partner and a pair of young sea-dogs.

So far his books have been nominated for the Carnegie Medal (twice), the Branford-Boase Award, and the Askews prize, as well as translated into Japanese and optioned for feature films.

OTHER TITLES IN THE RUNNING TIDE SERIES

Compass Murphy
Hunting Gumnor

STEPHEN POTTS

THE SHIP THIEF

EGMONT

To Miriam, GREYLAG, and Gail:
each very special in her own way

First published 2004
by Egmont Books Limited
239 Kensington High Street, London W8 6SA

ISBN 1 4052 0415 X

1 3 5 7 9 10 8 6 4 2

A CIP catalogue record for this title is available from the British Library

Typeset by Avon DataSet Ltd, Bidford on Avon, Warwickshire B50 4JH
Printed and bound in Great Britain by the CPI Group

'For most of my life I have messed about in boats, and at one point my home was a converted barge. I have lazed around in punts, paddled canoes, raced sculling boats and rowing eights, and sailed dinghies, yachts and tall ships on all kinds of water, from the Thames to the Caledonian Canal to the Arctic Ocean. I still get seasick.

This is a story about the sea and sea people: but it can only be told through their boats, for they are inseparable. It is dedicated, in part, to GREYLAG, a boat of my own, where much of it was written. She sails Northern waters now, where the geese she's named after wheel overhead and call to her, and where the whales and dolphins rise to her bow-wave. For these creatures know, as much as any sailor, how a ship can steal your heart.'

Stephen

CHAPTER 1
NORTHWARD BOUND

WATER LAPS WARM AT GIDEON'S ANKLES, heated by the sun-baked sand as the rising tide reclaims the beach. He wades deeper, till it's cool again, and makes for the shade of a rocky outcrop. Here he crouches, scoops up a handful of Pacific, and showers it on to his shoulders and his thick dark hair. He stands again, enjoying the brief refreshing chill the water brings, and turns till he faces north, and the open sea. The afternoon sun casts a short shadow before him as he gazes through the heat shimmer at the deeper, darker water beyond the wave-combed reef. He smiles.

Behind him, at the landward limit of the beach, his twin sister, Zannah, faces the opposite way, and peers into the shade of the jungle. She stands, as still as she can, hugged up close to a palm-tree trunk, and waits for

1

any monkeys – curious, hungry, or both – to explore the little gift of nuts she's laid out on a palm-leaf tray. While she waits she watches the rainbow flashes of parakeet wings flit between the trees beyond. And, high above, a monkey watches her. Curious *and* hungry it might be, but it is far too wary to approach while this human's about, so it settles down to outwait her.

A feathered flurry of reds and greens flashes through the canopy and startles the monkey. It leaps back, half-falling, and has to grab for a neighbouring tree, bumping a heavy coconut as it scrabbles to safety. The nut's stalk, stretched by the weight of the heavy husky fruit, desiccated by weeks of sun, tugged and twisted by sea breezes, finally gives.

Zannah knows nothing of this till the coconut cannons into the tree trunk behind her, and ricochets forward, hitting her in the shoulder with an impact like a horse's kick. She is hurled to the ground, her face slammed down into the leaves and sand, where she lies, stunned and breathless, gazing at the ants.

Gideon too is simultaneously flung forward by a blow to his shoulder. His face is plunged into the weedy water of the rocky foreshore, where he's suddenly staring at sea anemones and scuttling crabs. He splutters upright, and looks about for who, or what, has hit him, but sees nothing. Up on the beach a monkey screeches. 'Zannah!' Gideon shouts. Silence. There is no reply. He splashes out of the water, and runs up the beach.

His sister slowly gets to her feet, rubbing husk from her right shoulder. Beside her a new-cracked coconut tells its story, and beyond, unseen by Zannah, the monkey grabs her offering of nuts and scampers off.

When he sees she's unhurt, Gideon picks up the coconut and drinks from the dribbling milk. 'I felt it too,' he says. Zannah nods. They take for granted the fact each feels the other's pains, as if it is to be expected.

Gideon hands Zannah the nut but she shakes her head.

'I won't drink anything that's just tried to kill me. A bad omen with a long trip ahead.'

'Don't you want to go?'

'We're always *going*. I'd like to *be* somewhere.'

'Here?' Gideon gestures at the beach, the sea, the jungle.

'Why not?'

'For me the going is the best part. Better than just *being* somewhere.'

A distant bell sounds above the surf. The twins look at each other, then up at the sun, in an effort to estimate the time. And without a word they get up and run. Silky black hair – his curly, hers straight – streams behind, in parallel wakes. Sun-faded quilt-patch clothes flap wild in the breeze.

'We might get back –'

'– before they know.' Finishing each other's speech, as ever. Only now it is necessary: there's little enough breath for talk.

A distant whistle, shrieking impatience.

'Maybe not.' And two sets of steps quicken yet, as the beach gives way to a well-trodden track. Parrots and people scatter before their headlong rush. An old man trips over fishing nets, waving curses.

They hurdle upturned canoes. Bubbling mussels and still-wriggly crabs bounce from canvas bags, string-slung over their skinny shoulders. Neither looks back. The old man smiles at what they have left him.

Again the whistle, more urgently now.

'They wouldn't.'

'They might.' Ahead of them masts are in motion. 'For the devil of it.'

And on to the rickety pier, wood warm under bare running feet. The ship – *their* ship – is already unleashed, and a cleft has opened between ship and shore. A widening cleft, one that forces a choice. Go or stay. Run on or halt.

Their eyes meet briefly, sidelong, but there is no hesitation, no break in their stride: two decisions made in an instant.

A flying leap across sun-sparkled water towards the rigging of their departing home. Four hands grab for grip, four feet scrabble for purchase, but two of each come loose, and one berry-brown body falls, in an early autumn, with a shout and a splash, and a chorus of gasps from observers aboard and ashore.

The remaining berry looks from the tarry tree of the rigging, to the upturned faces on deck, and then down to the widening O of the ripples on the water, and jumps, to open another O nearby.

Captain Joshua Murphy watches from the helm, impassively. Everything about him is sparkly-dark. Lights gleam in his oil-black eyes, earrings flash against mahogany skin, sea-salt sprinkles his sailor's shirt, and grey flecks his dark curly hair. He hands the wheel to a crewman and bids him hold his course, then steps to the stern rail, where silence now reigns, and calls to the fish-children below: 'We'll be back in a year. Will you be here yet?'

A berry-fish shouts back: 'Aye, Father. For we'll swim in your wake till you haul us aboard.'

The captain is joined by Simva, his straight-haired

mate, who casts a line from the stern, as the ship gathers pace. 'And a long cold swim it would be, Joshua,' she says.

The twins splash after the wriggling rope. These fish are keen to be caught. When both are firmly hooked the line is drawn up, and they spill over the rail, streaming water and giggles.

'What a catch is this!' cries a crewman.

'Can we eat them?' asks another.

They are inspected, with grumbled proddings. 'Not enough flesh . . . Might be poison . . . The prettiest fish have most venom.'

And now the crew back off as the captain approaches. 'Welcome aboard, my little ship-jumpers.' He pulls his son to his feet. 'But we didn't know you had left.' And now his daughter. 'Which is why we did.'

Simva takes their canvas bags, writhing with seafood. 'It was only as we cast off we checked for you, and found you gone.' She bends, first to one: 'Why?' Then the other: 'Where?'

The twins, still out of breath, look first at each other, and then at their parents, captain and mate.

'The beach.'

'Rock pools.'

'Hot sand –'

'– between your toes.'

'Stripy fish.'

'Coconuts.'

'It would be the last time.'

'For *ages*.'

The straight-haired mate looks at the curly-haired captain. Her eyes are bright, but she does not smile. Not yet. Nor does he. 'And did you get one? A coconut, I mean,' he asks the twins.

Gideon nods, rummages in his bag, and pulls out the cracked husk. 'It nearly got us.'

Joshua weighs the nut in his hand, and flicks off the small green crabs that cling tenaciously to its hairy outside. When he sees that it's cracked, and that the salt water matting its husk has curdled the leaking milk, he hurls it into the ship's wake. He crouches, tousling first Zannah's wet hair and then her brother's. 'I made a similar leap, many years ago,' he says, 'across water much colder than this. I was embarking on a journey that would cost me dearly.' He gazes at the departing jetty, sadness in his eyes, till Simva takes his hand. He looks up at her: 'But it also brought me great joy.'

He stands again, a smile returned to his weather-beaten face. 'What we've just seen is that whatever journey you two make, you will make it together. Simva, can you say who it was who fell, and who jumped?'

His wife inspects the children for clues until, finding none, she shakes her head. 'No, I cannot.'

'Nor I.'

'But it matters not. Each would have jumped for the other.'

Joshua nods agreement. 'Exactly so.' He turns to the crewman at the helm. 'Let's shape our course, Mister Kanaka.' He pauses. All eyes swing to him, as if they are compasses, and he the pole. 'North.'

At the same stern rail, days later, the twins feel the first breath of cold, despite the early morning sun and the extra clothes they now wear. They know it's not just the brisk ship-driving breeze that chills them, but their increasing northness. Their mother stands beside them, staring towards the warm southern seas they are leaving. 'And what don't you see?' she asks.

'Birds.'

'Yes, Giddy. We're in Big Water now. Nothing but albatross for a month, I reckon, and then different birds altogether from the ones you both know.'

'Staaaaaarboard!' A raucous squawk from the left: a human word in the voice of a bird, still unseen. The twins smile. 'Oh I don't know,' said Gideon. 'There's always Pirate,' as the parrot squawks again the same command. Moments later it emerges into view, bobbing its rainbow head as it rides a precarious perch on the collar of a big black dog.

As the dog passes behind them the parrot calls once more, a different order now: 'Midships.' The dog halts and turns to face astern between the twins. 'All hands aloft!' and the dog raises his forepaws to the rail, stretching up on his hind legs so both he and the parrot can gaze on the brindled wake stretching away southwards.

Gideon and his twin each lay a hand on the dog's heavy head. He looks up at them in turn, and then, briefly, at the parrot. 'I know, Scoresby, I know,' says Gideon. 'There's just no peace, is there?'

'Orders orders orders, all day long,' says his sister, then turns to her mother. 'Will they be all right where we're going?'

'Alaska? Scoresby will. I think the parrot too. We won't go where it's really cold.'

'Why are we going at all?'

'We must trade, Zannah, that we may live. We stand on a ship full of spices, and hardwoods, and fine feathers, and silks. There is a call for such things up in Sitka now, and there we may load all the furs we can carry.'

'But why must we trade in the north?'

Simva turns round and bids her twins do likewise. The dog and parrot continue to stare wistfully southwards. Simva looks up at the towering masts, with their varnished spars gleaming in the sunlight, and the swelling canvas curves of the *Unicorn*'s full suit of sails driving the ship forward in the steady trade winds. She waves an appreciating arm.

'Every year more ships are launched without all this. They are built of metal and powered by engines. They are faster than us, they carry more cargo, and they go where they wish, not where the wind wants to take them.' She sighs. 'So every year trade is harder, for us and all sailing ships. Increasingly we must look elsewhere. It was me who chose the north. I have not seen it for years.'

'Will there be ice?' This from Gideon.

'No.'

'I want to see ice again.'

'As do I. But not from an old wooden ship that is our only home. We will not take her beyond Sitka.'

'Will there be bears?' asks Zannah.

'There are always bears in the north. It is their kingdom. We will show them the respect kings are due, and not approach too closely.'

The parrot knows nothing of bears and is bored by

this people-talk. 'All hands on deck!' he commands. Scoresby obeys with a sigh. Then 'Po-o-o-o-o-rt!' And dog and parrot continue their tour of the deck.

Gideon lies awake, enjoying the pendulum swing of his hammock. He listens to the creak of the ship's ropes and timbers, and the bubble and sigh of the sea running along the water-line wood a plank's thickness from his head. A moonbeam shaft drops from the skylight overhead and silvers the sleeping shoulder of his sister in the hammock next to his.

Curled in the corner, below them both, Scoresby twitches in his sea-dog dreams. His breath ruffles the feathers of Pirate, swinging on a nearby perch with his head tucked under the extravagant cloak of his wing. A single downy feather, platinum white, hangs in the air, puffed up and down with the dog's breath.

Two other feathers already adorn Scoresby's shoulders, where they stand out against his glossy black coat like snowflakes on coal.

'You turning into a bird?' Gideon whispers to the dog, who replies from his dreams with a stifled yelp, followed by a low growl. A long pink tongue slides over his bone-white teeth.

Maybe not, thinks Gideon. *Too much the dog still, even in your sleep. But perhaps you and Pirate are turning into something else altogether. A dog-bird, a bird-dog. You never see one without the other. Six legs, two wings, one voice.*

It was true: ever since Pirate came aboard in Tahiti three years earlier, he and Scoresby had been inseparable, and never more than the length of the ship came between them.

What was it Zannah said about you? Together forever whatever. Gideon turns to his sleeping sister. *Will it be like that for us?*

He stretches down and gently enfolds the airborne feather in his hand then reaches across to release it over Zannah's mouth, trying to get it to float on her breath as it had on the dog's. Instead, when he lets it go, it drifts down to her face. She brushes it away, and turns aside with a sigh.

Hungry twins cling to the mast, high above deck, as the ship rolls in the open ocean swell. Bells sound below. Eight of them. And then the familiar voice of Nathan, roaring up at them: 'There is food to be had here, which I will feed to dog and bird and fish if there are not people enough as wants it.'

12

'Yum yum.' Zannah's eyes sparkle as she and Giddy scramble for the rigging, he to port, she on starboard. 'Yum yum yum!' she shouts as she leads the race downwards. Her brother's struggling to keep up. Zannah's first to the lower yard, where she yells a challenge up to Giddy: 'Yum yum YAM!'

Nathan looks up at this, and at Giddy's defiant reply – YAM yum yum – as he scoots after her. They drop so fast they almost fall the last few feet to the deck. Nathan grabs an arm of each as their still-bare feet touch wood together. 'Halleluya!' he shouts, then laughs at their bemusement.

His huge encircling hands unclasp their skinny wrists, and he stoops to grin before them. 'Do you know what it means?'

'What what means?'

'That nonsense you yammered in the rigging.'

Zannah and Giddy shake their heads, as Nathan continues. 'Stick a "*Yeshly*" in front and a "*Halleluya*" astern and you've got a Hebrew fisherman's chant from Jaffa, as old as can be. *Yeshly yom yom yam*, they sing, as they haul in their nets. *Yeshly yam yom yom*. And then at the end, when the fish flop into the boat – *Halleluya!*

'*Every day we have the sea*, it means.' He stands to

stare ahead, at the endless lines of rolling waves. *'Every day the sea has us.'*

No longer held by his hands or his stare, the twins skip in opposite circles round the deck, yum-yum-yamming all the while. Nathan strolls to the galley where the ship's company are filling their dishes before sitting down on deck to eat. Rosa looks from the twins to Nathan, her husband. 'What have you started?' she asks. 'What have you done?'

Nathan shrugs. ''Twas nothing that started wi' me.' He sits down too, as Rosa fills pannikins with meat and potatoes at the stove beside her.

'Is it warm water songs that you teach them now, Nathan?' asks Simva, taking up two pannikins. 'Are you done so soon with our cold northern oceans?'

'I'll go where my ship goes, whatever the warmth of the water.' Nathan breaks some bread over his dinner.

'But what about your wife?' asks Joshua, as Simva hands him one of the pannikins and tucks into the other.

'I don't need to leave harbour to feel my Rosa blow hot and cold by turns.' Nathan's grin exposes his missing teeth.

Rosa hits him square between the eyes with a well-aimed crust of bread as Zannah skips past. Zannah catches the crust as it bounces off Nathan's head. 'Yum

yum YAM!' she shouts, and takes a huge bite.

'They had nothing else, did they?' Simva asks Nathan.

'Who?'

'Your Hebrew fishermen. Every day they had the sea, but that was all they had.'

'Is it not enough?'

'There was no place they could build houses upon, and grow crops – potatoes like these, perhaps. No place they could point to, and call Home.' Simva stirs her stew thoughtfully. 'Who ruled their land when you heard their song?'

'The Turks. Who rule it still.'

'And before them?'

'I know not.'

Gideon, who has read through the ship's library more than once, cuts in: 'The Romans.'

'Always others,' murmurs Simva. 'And their kin, the Jews, do they not wander the world, trading where they can, and always outsiders to the lands they visit? So it is with us. We are homeless wanderers of the sea. And to answer your question, Nathan, no, it is not enough. Not for me.'

Joshua has listened throughout, apparently intent on his meal. Simva turns to her husband, her eyes entreating him to speak. The twins watch him too, but he goes on eating as if unobserved, though he knows he's not. He spears his last potato and holds it up, as he pointedly turns away and wipes his mouth. 'A fine meal, Rosa,' he says. 'Is there more?'

Simva stands in the galley behind her twin dishwashers. She reaches over their shoulders to add two pannikins, bread-wiped clean of all food, to the teetering pile. 'We think it is time.'

Gideon turns. 'Time?'

'Today we cross the fiftieth parallel. As far north as Whitby, in England. And it will only get colder. So when you have done here we will open the cold weather clothing store.'

Zannah and Gideon's dishwashing gains a new vigour, but the pan-pile shrinks oh-so-slowly. At last they finish, dry their water-puckered hands, and follow their mother, climbing down through the fore hatch.

In the musty darkness of the hold they wait as eyes adjust. 'How long since . . .?' asks Zannah.

Simva thinks, and remembers. 'A long time. Long enough for what you wore then to be no use to you now. I hope we find something else.'

She opens doors, lifts lids, and rummages in dark

heavy chests, but to no avail. She pauses, and sits on an old spare sail. Immediately she's up again, urging Gideon and Zannah to join her in dragging the sail aside. She peers into the darkness beyond: 'Aha!'

A pile of heavy woollen clothing, dark and salt-mottled, lies, carefully folded, in the deepest recess of the store. Zannah creeps in to hand out the articles one by one. Moths flutter up, and strands of wool spill on to the deck: the top two layers are badly holed. Simva discards them at once, but inspects the rest with care. She unfolds a huge jersey with a heavy rounded neck. 'Nathan.' Then a smaller, lighter one with curling designs on the front. 'Kanaka.' Now a skirt, the hem edged with red embroidered roses. 'Rosa.'

She beckons her son forward, and holds against his shoulders a heavily patched shirt. 'Gideon,' she smiles, in memory as much as in giving.

'Whose was it before?' Gideon fingers the patches, and the worn cloth, bearing the marks of travel and adventure.

'Your father's.'

'It looks like it has been everywhere.'

'Almost. Iceland, Lofoten, Svalbard, the Bay of Baffin – but mostly Greenland. Your father and I spent years there together before you arrived.' She

17

turns the shirt round, checking for a repair she'd made long before.

'Look.' She holds it up to view: an area of darning and patches that cannot quite hide a jagged rent in one shoulder. 'A walrus tusk.' She traces the line of the tear with her finger, and recalls with a shudder the sudden surge beneath the kayak when the huge hideous beast attacked. 'Thankfully your father needed less stitching than this shirt – but you will know the mark.'

And they do – an L-shaped scar high on Joshua's left arm, long healed and only obvious because it never took a tan, but stood out white against his skin.

'It was his own fault. An angry walrus is not to be approached.' She hands the shirt over for Gideon to don – which he proudly does – while she digs deeper into this rich seam of clothing and history.

Zannah watches a smile spread over her mother's face as she tugs out and unfolds a brightly decorated fur-lined tunic. Simva holds it up against her, then gestures for Zannah to raise her arms, so she can slip the tunic over her head. Zannah enjoys the warm animal softness of the fur as it slides over her face. She fingers the embroidery that circles the tunic's neck and shoulders, and smiles up at her mother.

Simva's voice sounds fur-lined now. 'My mother

made this for me. If we had stayed in Greenland it would have been yours already.' Her smile slides away. 'But we left for warmer waters, and there was then no need.'

'You've not worn it since?'

'No. I was waiting to return.'

Gideon finishes rolling up his too-long sleeves and looks up. 'Why have you waited so long?'

His mother sighs. 'An illness brought by the white man – whaling men, like your father's father – laid waste to my people.' She sits down on the old sail, no longer wanting to dig up old memories. 'My father, my mother, the rest, all sickened and died, one by one. Those who survived withdrew their welcome to your father: and with my family gone it no longer felt like home to me, though I had lived there all my life.'

Simva gestures at the wooden walls that surround them, and the objects lying about the hold. 'So we left, to find this ship and the wandering life we now lead on her.'

'And now you want to go back?'

'To Greenland, no. To the north, yes. It is in my blood.' She looks from Gideon to Zannah, seeing them again, rather than the figures from long ago and far away that she has unfolded with these old garments. She lays a hand on each of them, and pulls them a little towards her. 'And I want to see if it is in yours.'

In the very bows of the ship, hemmed in by Nathan to one side and a Pirate-less Scoresby to the other, Zannah turns to face astern and looks up. In each hand hangs a tattered red and yellow flag on a short staff. She waits, as does Gideon in the crow's nest, for Nathan's signal. A wave of his hand, and Gideon raises his arms, showing that he has flags of his own. They are newer and brighter than Zannah's and they snap in the breeze as he holds his arms outstretched.

'R . . .' mutters Zannah. She stares intently as her brother lowers the right flag and raises the left. 'E . . .'

Gideon drops both arms, then raises them to the same position. 'E again.' Now he keeps the right still, and holds the left out horizontally. 'F . . . R E E F . . . reef!' shouts Zannah.

Nathan nods. 'Now ask him where.'

Tentatively, Zannah raises her own flags, and goes through a series of signal positions, slowly at first, but then with increasing sharpness. Her flags seem to flutter more confidently by the time she's finished. 'Good,' says Nathan. 'You learn well.' Gideon is already signalling back. 'Your brother too.'

Zannah calls out the letters again. 'W . . . E . . . S . . . T . . . West.' The next nearly foxes her, for it was not a letter at all. 'Two,' she says after a pause. 'M . . . I . . . L . . . E . . . S. Reef two miles west.' She puts down her flags and waves to Gideon, while Nathan beckons him down, their lesson done for the day. But Gideon is signalling still. He does not call back, and there is urgency now in his movements. This time it matters, and both Nathan and Zannah call out the letters as he waves them down. 'W . . . A . . . L . . . E. Whale!' Zannah wants to shout, but Nathan bids her hush. Instead she signals back – *where?* – her urgency reflecting her brother's. But he has given up with signals, and simply points, dead ahead.

Nathan and Zannah whirl round together: and gasp. For in the water ahead, blissfully oblivious of the ship's approach, lies the huge domed back of a monstrous whale. Grey waves wash white against his grey flanks, and water cascades down his sides, running over speckled patches, and the deep weals of squid-fighting scars. The whale still doesn't see, or hear the ship, and only three of the ship's company seem to have seen him. Four, if the helmsman is alert.

Gideon turns to see who is on the wheel. His father, the captain. *Of course* he knows: he has crept up on this

21

monster without a word to his crew. But no one on board can miss the whale once he spouts. A huge cloud of fishbreath spray rises before the bowsprit, and hangs in the air as the ship sails into its midst. Oily rain spatters all over Nathan and Zannah at the bow. Gideon, who is above the cloud – but only just – smirks: but even he cannot escape the stench. He coughs and retches like Hal and Jacques on deck. Joshua's prepared, with a face-scarf that hides his smile.

When Zannah next looks up, through watering eyes, she sees the whale's massive tail-flukes, hanging high over the water, and almost touching the starboard yard, as he dives. Above her Gideon watches, as entranced as she is; but Nathan has gone. He stands precariously on the bowsprit, clutching Zannah's flags by his shoulder like a harpoon. Red flags flutter where a harpoon blade would gleam.

Joshua laughs and shouts from the helm. 'Old habits die hard, eh, Nathan?'

Nathan drops his arm, as Joshua continues. 'But harpoons are only red after they strike, and we will be striking no whales. Not on my ship.'

Nathan returns to the deck, and hands back the flags. 'An old grey bull, I reckon. Big. Very big,' he calls back.

'Why?' asks Zannah as she fingers the frayed red cloth of the flag.

'Why what?' Nathan's already busy again, checking the lines that secure the anchor.

'Why no whales?'

Nathan looks back to his captain, then turns to Zannah. 'Hunting the whale brings wealth, 'tis true: but it also carries costs. And sometimes the cost is too high. It was a whale that did for your grandfather, while your father was no older than you are now. Some men might take against the beasts after that, and hunt them all the harder.' He sets down his work and glances again to the helmsman. 'But not him. He will not see them harmed.'

Nathan cranes his neck and looks upward. 'Any more, Giddy?'

He doesn't need to ask. Gideon has already scanned the horizon three times. He shakes his head.

'Keep looking, lad. They migrate up and down these coasts. And if we're seeing whales, we will soon see land.' Gideon scans again. He's unsure what he wants to see more.

Land comes first, and however much he wants to, it is not Gideon, but Rosa, who sees it before anyone else.

'Age has not dimmed your eyesight,' Simva tells her, with a smile.

Rosa looks at Nathan, mending sails on the deck nearby. He struggles to break a thread with his few remaining teeth, before giving up and using his knife. 'No,' says Rosa, 'but perhaps youth did.' Simva laughs.

Nathan pretends not to hear, and winks at Gideon, who's been watching his sewing, ever eager to learn. But Gideon now finds the pull of the look-out post stronger than any twine. He starts up the rigging, with Zannah ahead – again. She reaches the crow's nest before he does.

Zannah stares at the mist-dimmed shoulders of land hunched low on the Eastern horizon. She points, as Gideon climbs into the barrel beside her. 'Alaska!'

Together they will away the mist, but it is stubborn, and clings to the hills like a shawl. They watch, for an hour or so of steady sailing, but it seems the shore gets no closer, and then the mist wraps up their blue-grey hills completely. 'Not today,' says Zannah, as she clambers out to the rigging. Gideon shrugs and follows her. 'If not today, then not tonight. We won't go in under darkness.'

Both are wrong. With Captain Joshua navigating and his mate Simva at the helm, their ship slips closer.

The mist lifts and a bright silver moon rises above the mountains. Nathan's perched on the very end of the bowsprit, peering intently ahead, and Kanaka's at the shrouds, swinging a sounding lead and calling the depth every few minutes. 'Vaddom twelve . . . vaddom ten,' he sings.

Gideon and Zannah huddle midships, buried in the unfamiliar but welcome warmth of their new old clothes. They watch Hal, Jacques and Sven furl the sails above, one by one, to slow the ship down, till she's ghosting along. Gideon wonders when he will be allowed to go aloft at night.

Zannah touches the good-luck Knight's Head carved on a post beside her, and then the even-more-good-luck head of Scoresby, as he presses up close. She looks through a window at her father, concentrating hard over his charts and instruments in the galley, now doubling as the pilot room. 'He must be very sure.'

Gideon nods. 'He's always sure. Or if he isn't –'

'– he'd never let it show.'

'No. He never lets anything show.'

'Sometimes I wish he would.'

'Vaddom nine.' Kanaka's call brings them back to the task at hand.

'What are we to look for?' asks Gideon.

'Lights. The lights of Sitka.'

They peer ahead. There is a dull glow behind a headland, which seems to brighten as they approach.

'Vaddom ten.'

It is the only sound. The wind is light, and the ship's progress so tentative that there is barely a ripple at the bow, and none of the singing surge that hissed in their ears all the way from the South Seas.

'Listen,' says Gideon. Zannah closes her eyes, the better to concentrate. She shakes her head, and then her eyes pop wide as she hears it too – a low buzzing, or hum, as of distant bees. Voices.

The babble grows louder, and the glow brighter, as the headland draws closer, until, when they round it, they see and hear and smell the waterfront of Sitka, laid out before them in all its garish racket.

The little town is busy, and the harbour packed with vessels of all types, which carry lights and voices of their own. Rowing boats ply to and from the shore, and raucous shouts from all around affront the still of the night. Some of the shouts sound strange.

'Russian,' says Nathan. 'This used to be part of Russia once. It was never so busy then.'

There is shouting of their own, and a loud rattling of chains, as the anchor is lowered, once Simva's chosen her spot. The last sails are furled, and Hal and Sven make to unlash the boat.

Joshua calls them to halt. 'Later, I think. We will go ashore after a supper to mark our safe arrival.' Rosa's already busy in the galley.

Joshua draws Nathan aside, as the work goes on around them. 'There's something here I don't like. It's not the way I thought.'

'Nor the way I remember.'

'Just you and I in the boat when we go ashore.' Nathan nods.

Together they hoist a lantern into the rigging to show their ship's position.

Happy chatter rings round the dinner table. Joshua has opened the wine store and Rosa laid on one of her special meals. For the first time in a month the whole ship's company eat together, now they no longer need to stand watches. Even Pirate has shown himself, announcing his return with a new word.

'Spasibo,' he squawks, again and again.

Nathan sees Zannah frown at the bird. 'Thank you,' he says.

'For what?'

'It's Russian. He's picking up the local language already.'

'Maybe he means it,' says Hal. 'Thanking us all for getting across the Pacific in safety.'

Jacques picks up the banter baton. 'Ce n'est pas possible. 'E would not zank us for bringin eem to mingle viz bear and eagles, and so far North no parrot 'as ever bin.'

'Spasibo.'

'And zis still ze summer.'

Joshua smiles at his crew. 'He need not fear. As soon as we have finished our trading we will move on. Back to warmer waters.' He tries not to hear Simva's sigh. 'We will trade on the same basis as always. A third of the profit for the ship, then equal shares for all.'

'But there is one difference,' adds Simva. She and Joshua both turn to their twins.

'Yes,' says Joshua in a tone that will not hear debate. 'Now Zannah and Gideon take shares too.' The twins don't know where to look – except at each other.

Sven looks up from his plate, piled so high that no plate shows. He says nothing – he never does – but his meaning is clear enough.

Joshua addresses him directly. 'I know this means less for others. But they work watches and scrub decks and wash dishes, and as their father and their captain I will see them paid for it.'

Sven nods, silent still, and bends to his plate. No one else speaks either, as if Sven's quiet is infectious, until Hal looks at his shipmate's mountain of food. 'Even together they eat less than you, Sven.'

Another silence stretches, broken at length by the parrot: 'Dosvedanya.' Sven smiles, at the bird, and then at the twins, and finally at Joshua. Chatter builds up round the table once more like a fire taking hold: slowly at first, then, fuelled by wine and beef and bread, with gathering force.

When he judges the time is right, Joshua meets Nathan's eye. They slip away from the table, unnoticed by all except Simva.

Hal is holding forth. 'A ranch, way out west. As far as you can get from the sea, with horses, and a whole herd of steers. A log house, with an upstairs, and a fire always burning for a warm bath.' This thought quiets his crewmates. They haven't had a bath, warm or otherwise, for weeks. Hal sniffs his armpit, grimaces, and continues: 'And you, Jacques. How will you spend yours?'

'I spend it already.'

'Oh?'

'I 'ave debts. And I can never go 'ome till zey are paid.' He reaches for the bottle. 'One more trip.'

Rosa snorts. 'You've been saying that for four years, since you snuck on board at Marseilles. And you never yet said where you found your debts.'

'I never found zem. Zey found me.' He pours himself another glass.

'Sven?' Simva steers the talk around the table. Sven is the only one still eating, his red-blond beard matted with grease. She doesn't expect a response.

Sven wipes his lips with the back of one huge hand, belches loudly and takes a glug of wine. 'A summer house,' he announces. This time the quiet round the table comes from surprise, which Sven extends. 'To live in all year long,' he says, eventually, before letting out a huge laugh. No one joins in.

'I want a ship,' Gideon pipes up. 'A ship of my own, to go where I will.' He runs a hand over the dark heavy beam beside him. 'A ship like this.' When he looks up it is to see the sharp corrective in his sister's gaze. 'To go where *we* will.'

Zannah, conscious of her mother's eyes on her, looks out of the porthole to the lights of Sitka, deepening the darkness of the land beyond. When she turns back to face her brother, there is something of that darkness, and something of those lights, in her eyes. 'Then *I* will have a house. So *we* always have a home on land.'

Simva stares from one to the other, in a cool sizing up, a measuring of difference. She nods, just to herself, but says nothing. A silence spreads among the crew, but only briefly, for it is broken by an urgent bumping against the hull, then hurried feet on deck. Scoresby stirs, though the parrot does not. The galley door opens, spilling light on the anxious faces of Nathan and Joshua.

'All hands!' says Joshua. 'We're leaving.'

No one stirs.

'Now!' he snaps; and only then does his urgency infect the limbs of his crew and prod them into sudden movement.

Gideon and Zannah work a capstan beam together, raising the anchor as the sails are lowered. Joshua works the beam ahead, talking to his crew. 'There is a sickness here. A kind of yellow fever.' He waits for the name of this plague to visit its horrors on those who had seen, and survived, its workings. The capstan clunks, and the anchor chain rattles down the hawse-pipe into the chain locker deep in the bows. 'If we leave before daylight, we will not get caught for quarantine.'

'But leave for where?' asks Hal.

'I'm not sure, but with this cargo . . . I think Japan.' The capstan clunks for two full turns, as the men take in what this means: thousands of miles of the North Pacific, and all its storms. The twins hear quiet steady cursing, in his native Norwegian, from Sven on the beam behind them.

'Anchor up!' shouts Nathan, at the bow. The ship's begun to move. Joshua wants more sail, but he waits, and watches, as the crew gather at the stern rail, to see the lights of Sitka dimming, like their hopes, in their vessel's moonlit wake.

CHAPTER 2
A PLAGUE UPON US

SEA AND SKY ARE EMPTY OF EVERYTHING BUT different densities of grey. The smudged line where they meet undulates, breaks, and reforms. The crow's nest is empty too: what need is there for a look-out when land is so distant, when whale spouts will be ignored, when no ice comes this far south?

Giddy and Zannah stand at the port bow, hoping for a break in the clouds to dispel the gloom that's hung about the ship since their escape from Sitka. They've heard all the grumbles, doubts and regrets rising and falling among the crew as the Pacific swell rolls under their vessel, day after day.

'If it's the Far East we're headed for, how come we're sailing west?' asks Gideon, more of himself than his sister.

Zannah shrugs and says nothing. She's staring at the waves ahead.

Giddy persists. 'If you go far enough one way do you always end up going the other?'

Zannah frowns and stares harder. *Something white against the grey, far ahead and a little to port.*

'What about up? If you go far enough up, must you always come down?'

No, it's gone. Was it there at all?

'It's not true for down.' He too stares at the sea – the deepest in the world, Joshua had told them. 'So many ships. So far down. They never come back up.' He shivers and looks to his sister. What's she seen?

Yes – there! – sweeping low along the waves, dipping behind the bigger crests, then lifting clear to soar free.

Gideon follows Zannah's arm and sees it too. They watch together for a time, and then, while she marks it from the deck, he climbs to the crow's nest, where he lifts to his eye a battered brass telescope. He swings it towards the patch of sea-sky borderland pinned to the horizon by Zannah's finger. A moment to focus, another to steady and –

'Albatross!' he calls down. There had only been a handful since Tahiti, and none since Sitka, but there is no mistaking this one. Its boat-shaped body hangs

34

between huge wings, each as long as the twins are tall, to make a cross, sweeping low over the waves. Gideon knows there are sailors who would shudder at the sight, seeing it as a bad omen, but there is little superstition on the *Unicorn*, and none in him. He watches as the great bird wheels and glides along and between the waves, then lowers his brass eye.

Immediately he raises it again. 'There's something else!' Something below the bird, bobbing and passive and small.

'A boat! A boat!' he yells, turning to Nathan at the helm and pointing with his telescope. Nathan swings the helmwheel and curious crewmen put down their deck-work to come to the railing and watch. Simva emerges from the pilot house, Joshua soon after, a telescope more powerful than Gideon's in his hand. He stares down it a long cold time. 'My God,' he breathes eventually, and lowers the telescope. 'A boat indeed. And there are men in it. I cannot tell if they live.'

He gives orders to furl sails to slow the ship, and ladders are slung over the leeward side. Gideon gazes on from above. He counts the bodies sprawled in the bottom of the tiny boat. ' Four of them!' None move, and none have seen the ship. The albatross passes overhead, again and again; and as the cloud above thins, a faint cross-shaped shadow flits over the boat, and the men it bears, as if in a bird-borne blessing.

Jacques climbs carefully into the boat while Hal and Sven, hanging from the ladders, make fast at bow and stern. No one speaks, and all eyes follow Jacques as he bends over the four huddled shapes in turn. The boat is a mess. The remnants of a makeshift mast stand near the bow, in a tangle of splintered timbers, torn shreds of tarpaulin, and knotted ropes. The four bodies lie in grotesque positions, curled round empty barrels, bent over chests, squashed under seats. Seawater sloshes round the bottom of the boat, running over the sightless eyes and into the speechless mouth of the man who lies there. It is obvious he is dead.

Jacques points to him, and one other, further astern. 'Two of zem dead.' He indicates the remaining two, one of whom stirs slightly. 'And two of zem desperate.'

Joshua calls down. 'The logbook? A name?' It's hard to suppress the still-painful memory of finding his father's wrecked boat on a desolate Greenland beach, and, underneath, the frozen logbook, with its terrible tale of how he and his crew-mates met their end.

Simva looks across to Joshua, remembering too.

36

Throughout an Arctic night she had listened for bears, and held the burning brands by which Joshua first thawed and then read his father's last words.

'No logbook.' Jacques, in the boat, and Sven, at her bow, shake their heads. Hal runs a hand over the faded lettering on the stern. 'The *Bosky*,' he calls up.

At this the stirring figure opens salt-reddened eyes. He looks about at his rescuers, uncomprehendingly, and then at the albatross which still sweeps overhead. His eyes widen in fear, and his mouth opens to show purple bleeding gums. A hoarse unformed whisper is all that emerges. Jacques bends, the better to listen, but he has no need, for with a desperate effort the sailor speaks loud enough for all to hear: 'Beware the crow . . . Beware the crow.' All energy spent, he falls unconscious again.

Jacques checks his breathing. ''E 'as gone mad, I zink.'

'Hard enough to stay sane, after such an ordeal,' says Joshua. 'We will bring him and the other survivor on board, then sink the boat with the bodies.'

Hal looks up. 'No burial?'

Joshua shakes his head. 'I will not bring fever aboard this ship for the sake of dead men's souls.' He pauses. 'Will you speak for them at the sinking?' *For I cannot,* is left unsaid.

Hal looks at Jacques then back up to Joshua. 'I will, though I am no priest.'

Simva speaks for the first time since the boat has been sighted: 'As will I.'

The two sunken-eyed survivors are lifted gently from their boat, passed up the ladders, and lowered on to the deck. Where it is not burned brown by wind and sun, and streaked silver by salt, their skin is a wrinkled yellow-grey, like old parchment. As if trying to read it, Rosa lays a hand on each brow, and shakes her head. 'I feel no fever,' she says. 'But we must get water into them.'

She passes a cloth to Zannah, and bids her dip it in the water barrel, then hand it back. Rosa holds the dripping cloth above one mouth, then the next, dribbling water past cracked and swollen lips, drop by drop. Neither man swallows, and a trail of bloodstained froth runs down one man's chin to bury itself in his unruly beard. Rosa looks up. 'They've drifted a long time.'

'Aye,' says Nathan. 'But from where? There's none bar us in these waters.'

Rosa wipes the cloth across each man's lips. 'If

we nurse them well – and we shall – they will tell us soon enough.'

Joshua turns aside, to see the helmwheel unattended. 'And meanwhile we must be putting miles behind us,' he says. Nathan follows his glance, and returns to his post, as his crew-mates climb to unfurl the sails.

The ship is soon under way once more, the battered boat with its terrible cargo towed alongside. When all the sails are set, and the course steady, the crew gather at the taffrail. Scoresby – minus Pirate – looks on from afar. Jacques takes an axe and drops down into the boat once more. He pretends he's not unnerved by talk of fever, and insists it must be him who goes. Hal flicks through a prayer book, in search of words that might sound right.

Jacques stands astride the body in the bottom of the boat, and after a glance up to Hal and Simva, he swings the axe down hard – once, twice, three times – on the timbers either side of the keel, trying not to look at the men to whom this boat had first spelt salvation, and later the slowest and harshest of deaths.

Water rushes up through the jagged rents his axe-strokes leave, as if to reclaim what it owns, and Jacques steps back on to the ladder. With two more swings of his axe, at bow and stern, the retaining ropes are severed, and the boat drifts behind as it settles in the water. Hal snaps the book shut and speaks, in words all his own.

'We know them only as two sailors, who now meet a sailor's end. We know not their names, their countries, nor who might grieve for them but us. And now we consign them to the deep, knowing that there, but for the grace of God, go we, and all in peril on the sea.' Hal is indeed no priest, and these, his words, no prayer: but everyone says 'Amen'.

Little of the boat shows above the water now. A barrel floats free, is filled by a wave, and sinks. The dead hand of the dead man at the bow moves, with the waves, as if in farewell. Gideon hears Zannah catch her breath.

Simva stands behind her children, watching with them, and begins to speak – but in Inuit, not English. Zannah and Gideon know enough to pick out odd words, but not enough to understand. They look to Joshua, who understands it all, to fill in the gaps, but he won't look back. Simva signals she has finished, with a second 'Amen.'

The boat, and all in it, are gone. But in the sky above the bird soars still.

Speculation circles the table along with bowls of stew. Although it is still cold, and now dark, Pirate has emerged, as he always does at mealtimes, for company, warmth, and begged or stolen morsels. Not even Pirate could keep Scoresby from his dog-bowl outside; so now the bird sits on Zannah's shoulder, eyeing the bread.

Everyone but Pirate looks up when Rosa enters. 'They rouse a little,' she says, taking up a bowl. 'I may even get some broth into them.'

Simva stands, and waves Rosa into her seat at the table. 'I'll go,' she says. 'You've been there all day.'

Zannah stands up sharply, surprising Pirate. 'Me too?' she asks.

Simva hesitates, looking to Rosa and Joshua. 'To the window, yes. Through the door, no.'

Pirate doesn't want to go outside, but Zannah's out on deck before he can find a substitute shoulder, and his way back is closed against the wind as Simva emerges, a bowl of broth and bread in her hand, and the door is shut behind her.

A few steps take Zannah to the window of the carpenter's – Nathan's – workshop, where benches have been cleared and hammocks hung for the men plucked from the boat. Zannah presses up against the glass, squinting into the dim light and the looming shadows

cast by the single candle within. She can make out – just
– the faces of the two men, a little less ravaged than
when they came aboard that morning.

The candle flickers, to make the shadows jump,
when Simva opens the door. She squeezes between the
hammocks, and wafts the bowl under each man's nose.
The man who had spoken of crows stirs a little, the
other hardly at all. She lowers a chunk of broth-soaked
bread to the first man's mouth. A flurry of coughing and
splutters tells her he's not ready yet.

She tries the other man, who takes a little. She
pauses, then tries some more, but his mouth is now tight
shut. She bends to place the brimming bowl on the
bench, and outside, on Zannah's shoulder, the parrot
speaks: 'Beware the crow!'

Zannah sees the man's eyes flicker open, slide
sideways, and then quickly close as Simva stands up, this
time with the candle in her hand. Simva turns to the
window with her finger to her lips, but Zannah's already
cupped a silencing hand round the parrot's head.

Zannah watches as her mother studies the man. She's
counting his breaths, which are steady and slow. She
reaches for the pulse at his wrist, but frowns on finding
nothing. She tries his neck, fingers laid on a scarf he's
tied there. Again she frowns. She makes to undo the

scarf : but the man's hand shoots out like a striking snake and grabs her wrist. Simva within, and Zannah without, both step back, startled. The man's eyes are wide open now. No one speaks. Even the parrot senses the need for silence.

As the man takes in Simva's shock, he releases his grip, and tries to calm her with a smile that doesn't reach his eyes. Weakened though he is, there's a fierceness, a cruel intelligence in his look that makes Zannah wary. 'Forgive me,' he croaks, in English, with an accent hard to place. 'Maria tied it there. I vowed no other woman's hand would remove it.' Another quick smile as he struggles to sit up, enlisting Simva's aid.

'You must eat,' she says, proffering the bowl. 'There will be time to talk later.'

He takes it greedily, listening while Simva recounts his rescue. She doesn't mention the dead crew-mates. When the broth is gone, and the story done, his eyelids droop as fatigue washes over him once more. He struggles against a tide of tiredness. 'Call me Vincent,' he says. His head lolls to the right as he looks at his companion. 'He's Michael. Has he spoken?'

'You must rest.'

'Has he spoken?'

'Something about a crow, when we found you. It

made no sense. There's been nothing since.' Simva takes the empty bowl, and lowers the candle to the bench. 'Rest now. We will bring more broth later.'

Vincent's eyes give up the struggle and close, as Simva leaves, but something makes Zannah watch on. Moments after the door clicks shut, his eyes spring open, as he turns to face Michael, all traces of drowsiness banished in an instant. Zannah feels a chill of fear as he looks sharply around the room. She steps quickly back from the window, not sure what she has just seen, or what it means.

'His name's Vincent.' Zannah's scrubbing the deck. She pushes the heavy brush towards her brother. 'And I don't like him.'

Gideon pushes the brush back. 'Why not?'

'I don't know.'

'You must have a reason. Has he spoken to you?'

'No.'

'Looked at you?'

'No.'

'Do you know *anything* about him?'

'Yes.'

'What?'

'I know that I don't like him.'

Gideon gives up, and scrubs on in silence. The workshop door opens and a troubled-looking Rosa emerges. She makes straight for Joshua at the helm. Kanaka and Sven break off their sail-mending as she passes, but the twins scrub on.

'And the other one?'

'Michael? He's not talking.'

Kanaka walks to the stern. Without a word he takes the helm as Joshua steps forward and returns to the workshop with Rosa, an arm around her shoulder. Sven joins them at the door. His heavy sail-maker's needle hangs from the coil of stout twine in his hand. It glints in the sunlight as they pause to compose themselves before they go in. The door is closed firmly behind them.

Gideon and Zannah lay their brush aside and wait, exchanging questioning looks. Eventually the door opens again, and Sven and Joshua struggle out, with a muttering Vincent, still in his hammock, borne between them. Gideon and Zannah strain to hear his mumbles, as the hammock is rigged between main mast and capstan, to swing in the open air. They catch a few words each time he swings towards them: 'My oldest friend . . . A stout heart . . . Poor Michael.'

While Joshua disappears below and Sven returns to

the workshop, Rosa steadies the hammock to offer Vincent water and soft words. 'At least he went peacefully. A better end than your companions in the boat.'

Vincent mutters again. 'The boat . . . Oh God . . . The boat.' His head rolls from side to side. 'So many days . . . and then the nights . . . That damnable bird.' Gideon scans the skies – but the albatross is gone.

Joshua soon returns, bearing two heavy rocks, taken from the ballast in the hold. He joins Sven inside the workshop.

Vincent's seen this, and his muttering's suddenly stopped. He fixes Rosa with his fierce gaze: 'Am I now sole survivor?'

She nods.

'And this ship is?'

'The *Unicorn*. Bound for Japan.'

He slumps back, muttering again. Rosa offers more water. 'Please rest. And drink.'

Zannah's crept, unnoticed, to the workshop window, and Gideon to the door. They watch Joshua place the rocks on the body in the hammock, down where the feet stick up, then pull the rough canvas edges of the hammock towards each other. Sven's sharp steel needle flashes, as he sews the edges together, to turn the hammock into a shroud. They work quickly and quietly upward, from feet to knees to hip, and up to the unbreathing chest, careful to touch the hammock and the dead man it contains as little as they can. Joshua lifts a clenched hand from its claw-like grip on the hammock edge. He has to hold down the arm, already stiffened in death, while it is sewn in place.

Sven hesitates when his stitching reaches the neck. He stares at the tight grey face, and the dark fearful eyes, still open, staring sightlessly up. 'Fever?' he asks.

Joshua shakes his head, and lowers the dead man's eyelids. 'I think not. He shows no signs. And he had begun to recover.' He pulls the last of the canvas across and Michael's face is gone.

Sven stitches on. 'Then what?'

Again Joshua shakes his head. He glances through the open door to see Vincent swinging outside, and the twins staring. He waves them away and looks up at Sven as the last stitch slides through, and the knot is tied. 'I don't know, Sven. I don't know.'

Michael's body lies in its rough wrapping on a plank balanced between the ship's rail and the hatch cover.

The crew stand around, careful not to get too close. This time it feels more like a funeral: and this time it is Joshua who holds the book.

He offers it to Hal, who shakes his head: 'I spoke for his shipmates. I cannot speak for him.' Sven stares straight at the sea, Nathan at the sky. Jacques studies his boots. Kanaka's busy at the helm. Joshua sighs and opens the book. But it is not he who speaks.

'In the midst of life we are in death.' It is Vincent, sitting up in his hammock, with a voice stronger and clearer than it has any right to be. Everyone turns. His gaze picks them out, one by one, as he recites the burial service.

'For as much as it hath pleased –' he coughs – 'For as much as it hath pleased Almighty God of his great mercy . . .'

Gideon sees Zannah shiver when Vincent's stare lights upon her. After the briefest of pauses, he continues, but only after she's looked away: '. . . to take unto himself the soul of our brother here departed . . .' Gideon steels himself: but when the dark eyes swing past him he feels no fear, and sees in them nothing but sadness for a lost crew-mate.

Vincent's staring at the lifeless body in the canvas cocoon. He signals that Sven and Jacques, standing ready by the inboard end of the plank, should lift and tilt it up.

'Ashes to ashes. Dust to dust. We came from the water, and return there we must.' With that the heavy shape slides quickly down the plank and drops into the foamy bow-wave speeding past below. Any splash it raises is soon lost in the swirling wake. Gideon and Zannah are both astonished at how fast all trace has vanished. It is as if Michael was never there at all.

Already Joshua's busy. He hands his book to Nathan, and makes for the galley, soon returning with a steaming urn, a block of soap, and a scrubbing brush. He strips to the waist, hurls his shirt into the sea, and sets about scrubbing his hands and his arms. 'I want everyone who touched him to clean themselves as never before. Then we'll do the same to this plank and the workshop. If this was fever I want it passed to none of us.'

''Twas no fever.' Vincent's still sitting up.

'Oh? You may bear it too.'

'His heart gave out. I heard him in the night, raving in his delirium, yelling about a crow.'

Zannah frowns. She'd heard nothing, and she'd lain awake much of the night, troubled by what she'd seen in Vincent's eyes the previous evening.

'I tried to comfort him, but at the height of his raving

49

he fell abruptly silent, and I knew that he was dead.'

Zannah looks to Rosa, another light sleeper who berths nearby, and sees her frown too.

Vincent appeals to them all. 'If you doubt me, and you fear fever yet, I will nurse myself. No, I will do more. Quarantine me: lock me back within the cabin. I will scrub it down for you. All I ask is water, and bread, and a little salt beef. If, three days hence, I still live, you may be sure I have brought no pestilence aboard your ship.'

Everyone looks to Joshua. He pauses in his scrubbing, stares at Vincent, and nods.

A put-upon Scoresby approaches the bowsprit. His ears quiver in the breeze and wrap around the tightly curled toes of the parrot on his collar-perch. 'Ready about!' Pirate squawks, and the dog turns round, back towards the company of the twins.

'It must be getting warmer,' says Gideon.

'I don't feel it,' his sister replies.

'Nor me.' The sun is out, but they're both in cold-water clothing still.

'Heave to!' commands the parrot. The dog sits down, looking mournfully up at each twin in turn, as if begging to be rid of his multi-coloured jockey. Pirate bends to

Scoresby's ear, like a rider to his horse, then takes it in his beak and nibbles gently. The dog pretends not to like it.

'If it's no warmer Pirate must have grown more feathers.'

Zannah holds out a peanut, still in its shell. Pirate quickly grasps the proffered nut in one claw, and tears it open with his beak. Fragments of shell fall on the velvet tip of Scoresby's ear. He doesn't notice.

Gideon does, and brushes them off. 'Still, it's nice to see them together.'

'Mmm.' Zannah rummages in her pocket for another nut.

'Especially now Albert's back.'

'Albert?'

'Yes. Surely you've seen him.'

'Albert who?'

'He travels as widely as we do. We've met loads of his family.'

'What are you –'

'The Rosses. They're everywhere. A far-flung clan. All the way from Scotland.'

'I don't –'

'Think about it.' Gideon looks up and astern. A familiar bird sweeps along the far horizon.

Zannah follows his gaze. 'Albert Ross?' Finally she gets it. 'Albatross!' She lunges at him. 'I'll get you!'

But Gideon is ready. He skips out of her reach, and scurries off, with Zannah and a bemused dog-parrot in close pursuit. He dodges and twists round capstan and mast, jumps over hatch covers, and swings from the rigging, taunting her all the while. 'Have you met Albert's friends? There's Dolly Finn . . . and Jelly Fish . . . and –'

A dog behind his knees, and a quick push from Zannah combine to have Gideon crash to the deck, where he sprawls, winded, and disabled by laughter. Zannah seizes her chance and pins him with her knees. 'What's that?' she shouts, pointing off to the West.

'What's what?'

'That!'

He sees it now. A bird much smaller and more delicate than Albert, but with a flight just as effortless. 'It's . . . It's . . .'

She cuffs him lightly: and starts to laugh along with him. 'I'll tell you what it is. It's my Tern.'

Gideon wriggles and writhes to get free, but Zannah's only a little lighter than him, and just as determined. His feet thrash noisily, and in vain, till they connect with something made of wood and metal and send it spinning across the deck with a clatter.

'Hey there, you two!' chides Nathan. 'Enough.'

Gideon and Zannah untangle themselves and fall quiet when they see what it is they've hit: a gun. Nathan retrieves the lightweight pistol from the scuppers and lays it back on the hatch cover, alongside two long-barrelled rifles and another, heavier pistol. One rifle is partly in pieces, but the others, all intact, gleam brightly with pungent gun oil from the rag in Nathan's hand.

Gideon stares. He's never see them all together like this.

'Aye,' says Nathan gruffly. 'It pays to be quiet and careful wi guns about, eh?' He jerks a thumb in the direction of Vincent's workshop berth. 'And we've a guest who'd value some peace, an' all. So go easy, will ye?'

Zannah nods her agreement and points to the weapons. Scoresby follows her finger and bends to sniff the oily objects. 'What are you doing with them?'

'Checking. And cleaning. We use them so little – thank God – I can scarce remember where they are kept. But salt water and damp air don't treat gun metal kind, so they need oiling every so –'

Scoresby learns to his cost that he doesn't like the taste of gun oil. He recoils as sharply as if the gun had

53

gone off, prompting a shrill shriek and a sudden flurry of wings from Pirate. There's an angry knocking from Vincent's cabin.

Nathan bends close to the twins. 'You're best out of the way for a while. Vincent's getting irritable now his quarantine's nearly up.'

Gideon lays an outstretched finger against Scoresby's neck. A still-flustered Pirate edges sideways on to it, without even a glance at his unreliable mount. Gideon lifts him to Zannah's shoulder, where he readily takes up his perch, his rainbow feathers especially bright against the glossy sheen of her black hair. Gideon leads Scoresby astern, along the port rail, while Zannah takes Pirate to starboard. They meet at the taffrail, looking over the Unicorn's arrow-straight wake.

There's a silence, while they both watch the albatross, close on the port quarter. Neither wants to talk about guns, or about Vincent. Zannah gazes East, down the line of the wake, to where the Alaskan coast lies far below the horizon. She's aware that although they saw little enough of it, she and her brother know a great deal more about where they've been, than where they are headed.

She turns to him. 'Do we have books about Japan?' In her years of ocean-wandering the Unicorn had acquired a library of sorts, a random assortment of battered books, which had been the source for the twins' wide ranging but patchy education.

'I think I saw one.'

'What's it like there?'

'There's a big volcano, with snow. The people live in tiny paper houses. The men carry big swords, and they wrap the women up in yards and yards of silk.'

The albatross soars overhead to its station on the opposite quarter.

Gideon continues. 'Their writing's spindly squiggles, up and down the page, like inky starfish. But the thing I remember most is that they don't like foreigners.' He wondered silently if this was why Nathan got the guns out. 'They call them – us – gyjeen.'

There's a pause, before Zannah replies. 'But we're gyjeen wherever we go.'

It was true. Half-Yorkshire, half-Inuit, and not accepted in either place, she and her brother have wandered the world, and seen more of it than most: but every port and island and coast they land at belongs to other people: and even if they are welcomed, they are always only guests.

'It would be good to have somewhere we weren't foreign at all. Somewhere to call home. Somewhere we weren't just *visiting*.'

Gideon taps the rail. 'This. This is home. This is where we belong. Wherever the *Unicorn* is.'

Zannah turns to face her brother, suddenly animated. 'Where were you born?'

Gideon's taken aback. 'Same place as you. Well, almost.'

'Which was?'

'The South Atlantic.'

'Exactly. The middle of nowhere.'

Gideon shakes his head. It's his turn to be animated. 'If you want to know *exactly*, it was twenty-one degrees and fourteen minutes south, two degrees and twenty-two minutes west. A week past the African Cape, headed for St Helena.'

'You know that?'

'It's in the ship's log. In the captain's hand. You were born half an hour earlier, and a few miles south-east. We were running fast in the trade winds. At *exactly* –'

Zannah holds up her hand. 'Can I ever go back? Can I ever point to the patch of water, and *know*, without a chart, that it was there?'

'Why would you want to? It's a big ocean.'

'*Exactly*. Sometimes I wish it was just a little patch of land.' She turns back to face astern, as the albatross sweeps past again. 'Even Albert has to land sometime. He came from a nest, on a shore somewhere, and he'll go back to the very same place to make a nest of his own, with a Mrs Albert, and there'll be eggs and more Alberts to follow. We don't have that.'

They fall quiet, staring at the heavy clouds beginning to mass on the horizon, against which the albatross, lit by the afternoon sun, looks all the whiter.

Silence shatters as a gunshot cracks above and behind them. The soaring shape suddenly crumples. Gideon whirls round to see Vincent, reloading a newly cleaned rifle. Zannah never stops gazing at the stricken bird. It seems to hang in the air for a moment, before it spirals down to the sea, leaking feathers and blood. When it hits the surface one wing flutters for a time, before a second shot stills it, to leave the broken corpse riding the reddening water.

Now Zannah turns too, to see Joshua hurl Vincent aside and wrestle the gun from his grip. He makes to strike him with the gun's stock, but Vincent makes no attempt to defend himself, and Joshua pulls the blow back. Simva hurries up, with Hal and Nathan, all armed. Sven looks on impassively from the helm.

'What is this?' shouts Joshua. 'To fire on a defenceless bird, from the deck of my ship, with my gun –'

'– and over the heads of *my* children.' Simva turns on Vincent furiously.

The tight-faced effort it takes Joshua to control himself is obvious. 'It is all I can do not to turn this gun on you. Explain yourself, or I will lock you in that fevered workshop for our entire passage.'

Vincent stands entirely still. If he's afraid he doesn't show it, and when his voice comes it is quiet, but steady.

'I bid you still your anger, Captain Murphy, till you hear me out.' He turns to Simva. 'I am a good shot, as I have just shown, and I would never put your young ones in peril.' Only now does he look at the twins, and meet their shocked but challenging glare. He smiles thinly. 'However much their noise annoys me.'

He's talking to them all now. 'It grieves me to kill as I have, especially when it is not for food: but it would grieve me much more to fail in my promise to poor Michael, as he died.' He points at the water-borne clump of feathers, already distant. 'That accursed bird followed first our ship and then that boat for days – no, weeks – from one disaster to another. Michael came to see it as his death shadow. You heard him call it his crow, though all can see it is white.'

'Was,' said Hal. 'You have painted it red.'

Vincent stares at Hal, who grips his rifle tighter. 'I

vowed to Michael that if I survived I would kill the bird so that he might find peace. It was after that he slipped away. Condemn me if you will. I cannot stop you. But if you will have me join your table tonight I will tell you what befell us.'

After a long pause the guns are lowered, one by one, and without a word Vincent walks through the knot of people on the quarterdeck to the workshop, where he closes the door on their still-shocked faces. They stare on for a time, at the mute and answerless workshop walls, then turn aside to their tasks.

Nathan collects the guns. Both twins detect the smell of burned gunpowder that hangs round the rifle Joshua hands over, the one Vincent had fired. 'More cleaning needed, I think,' mutters Joshua. Nathan nods grimly.

The twins turn away, and stare astern, unsettled. There is nothing to see of the dead bird: and now the evidence of its killing is to be wiped from the gun by Nathan's oily rag.

CHAPTER 3
SHIPWRECK

THE GALLEY IS FULL OF PEOPLE BUT ALMOST empty of talk. Only Hal, Jacques and Simva are absent, for someone must work the ship: but these three chose their watches to avoid Vincent, whose silence infects those around him even if his fever does not.

His plate is wiped clean, slowly, and carefully, with chunks of new-baked bread. He sees Gideon do the same, and fixes him with a gaze.

'What's the worst danger at sea?' he asks, abruptly.

Silence deepens. Vincent's steady stare makes clear only Gideon is meant to reply.

Gideon blusters. 'A storm that – that comes on quickly, before you –'

Vincent lowers his gaze. There's a shake of his head

and swipe of his bread, for each dread danger that Gideon goes on to name.

'Pirates? . . . Uncharted rocks? . . . Shipworm?'

Gideon pauses. He doesn't like to name the last. 'Mutiny?'

Vincent looks up now. His eyes narrow, just for a moment, but he shakes his head once more. 'No, lad. There will be no mutiny on a well-run ship.' He takes a bite of his bread, till he's left with the crust, and looks about, more at the walls than the crew they enclose. 'Such as this. And the other hazards you list, though real enough, are mere trifles when set against – fire. Fire at sea, boy, that's the worst.'

He holds up the overdone crust, as if it is a charred timber from his dead vessel. 'That's what did for the *Bosky*. Out of Sitka we were, headed North. Short-handed, with a patched-up crew. So the cook took turns up the mast with the rest of us. A squall hit hard and fast, and we raced aloft to take in sail. The cook had lit his galley fires not long before. The captain wanted bread, you see . . .'

Vincent's looking round the room again, but at people now. His eyes settle on Joshua a little longer than the rest. And then on to Rosa.

'But that cursed cook forgot to damp the fires. So

when our sail handling was done and next we looked down it was to see black smoke and orange flame a-dancing from the galley door.'

Zannah tries to picture the same thing in their own galley. She shudders.

'We were on to it fast enough, and soon snuffed it out. But the damage was done. Burning pitch had dropped through the deck. We had fire in the hold.'

He lays the crust aside to look blankly ahead, as if seeing again the flames, breathing once more the tarry smoke, and reliving the desperate fight to save his ship. 'Two whole days we drifted as we fought it. An ocean of water lay all around us, but at the heart of our ship burned a hungry fire we could not reach to douse. Slowly we were forced astern. When the foremast went – and two men with it – we knew the game was up. We floated the boats and stocked them with such water and salt beef as we could rescue. When the second night came on and the flames lit up the empty sky we abandoned ship. But we stayed nearby, watching her burn down to the water-line, till dawn.'

'We argued about where to go. West, to Russia or Japan? East to Alaska? North to the islands? But it was the wind that chose, and sent us South for day after day after day, till first the beef was gone, and then the water, and then, one by one, my shipmates.'

He looks at the twins, hesitates a moment, and goes on. 'We agreed no cannibalism, though some argued for it. When the first two died we threw them overboard. After that we had no strength to do the same. And so we were, when you found me – us – on the point of death ourselves.'

His eyes flash briefly at Nathan and Joshua. 'And every mile we made was tracked by your precious bird.'

There's a long silence, made louder by the creak of the timbers, the ripple of the water along the hull, and the rustle of wind in the sails. Zannah studies Vincent, now that he's bent to the table. Her doubts have dwindled, but are not yet dead.

Joshua breaks the silence at last. 'An ordeal I cannot imagine, or even guess at . . . But I have a question.'

Vincent's immediately alert and on his guard.

'You mentioned boats. We found only one.'

'There were two. The third burned before we could launch it. Six of us in ours, seven in the other. We were separated in the first storm. Who knows their fate? The cook was among them, so I –'

Sven breaks in. His words are rationed, unlike his food, so he's very direct. 'You sailed north from Sitka. Where? And why?'

Vincent seems genuinely surprised. 'But surely you know? Are you not just out of Sitka yourselves?'

Nathan catches Joshua's eye: but neither need speak, for the door swings open, framing Hal against a lumpy twilit sea. 'Wind's rising, Joshua,' he announces. Only then does Gideon hear the changed wind tone in the rigging that tells of a blow coming on. 'I'd say we need to reduce sail now, before the night thickens more.'

A relieved Joshua stands to don his oilskins. 'Aye, Hal. You and your watch-mates must eat now. We'll attend to the canvas.'

There's a sudden bustle in the crowded cabin, as the warm and dry and well-fed venture out, to make way for the cold and wet and hungry. Vincent sees the coolness in Simva's eyes as she enters. He vacates his place at the table, and turns to Nathan at the door. 'I'll take a turn, if I may,' he says.

Nathan's unsure, but Jacques, who is already eating, hands over his oilskins. 'I zink you will need zese tonight. I 'ope to go wizout a while. You will find me in my bunk after I eat.'

'Are you strong enough yet?' asks Nathan, as he and Vincent leave together. Vincent's look is answer enough.

Jacques' mouth is full of potato, but Zannah understands, when he grunts and points to his sou'wester hat. Zannah slips from her seat, sweeps up the hat, and makes for the door, beyond which, out on deck, Vincent dons his borrowed waterproofs. Neither he nor Nathan hear the door open behind them, engaged as they are in a low muttered conversation. Zannah hears only the word 'Sitka' before Nathan grows more insistent and audible.

'Such talk turns heads,' he says. 'And that turns ships.'

Vincent buttons up his jacket and nods. 'All right,' he agrees. 'I'll say nothing.'

It's then he notices Zannah, who hands over his hat. He clamps it firmly on his head and swings easily up into the ratlines, then climbs into the overhead darkness. Zannah watches him, as he ascends, his form dimming against the sky. *Say nothing about what?* she ponders.

Gideon peers over the edge of his swinging hammock. 'Not this again,' he groans. 'Please.'

Zannah stands in the corner, braced against the roll and pitch of the ship, as she unties the foot end of her own hammock. She has to squint in the dim light cast by a bucking oil-lamp. 'Why does it bother you?'

'It just does.'

'You know I do this when the wind gets up.'

'I could hardly not know, could I? But I don't know *why*.'

'I've told you.'

'Yes, yes, I know what you *said*: "She pitches more than she rolls above a Force 7 –"'

'– And this is an eight. At least. So I turn my hammock sideways on.'

'It's just that I don't believe you. And nor does Scoresby.' The talk and the movement has woken the dog, who's crammed into his bumpy corner, whining miserably. The parrot, on his pendulum perch, doesn't stir his head from under his wing.

'All right. Maybe I *feel* the pitch more than the roll. Maybe I *prefer* the roll to the pitch. What does it matter to you?'

'Because.'

'Because nothing.' She reties her hammock athwartships, below and at right angles to her brother's. A break in their talk allows each to register the noises outside and above: the shouts to and from the helm, the roar of the waves, the hiss of their spray, and the rising moan of the wind in the rigging. Neither really wants to hear, however many storms they've ridden through, so the banter must start again.

It's Gideon who takes it up. 'I don't think it is anything to do with the angle. It's that you tie it lower down.'

'But I only tie it lower down because you're in the way higher up.'

'I don't call trying to sleep in my usual place being in the way – but even if I am, it's the being lower down that makes you feel the movement less.'

At this, as if to test his theory, the ship begins a roll that's different from the rest: more sudden, more violent, faster. Zannah holds on, and tries not to raise her voice. 'Look, I'm not asking you to –'

She breaks off when the roll does not. The ship heels ever further over on to her port side, till the outboard wall, with its porthole, becomes the floor. Black water and grey foam rush past the fragile glass, wanting in. Clothes and books, plates and mugs, model ships, a spyglass and more fly about the cabin, knocking a terrified Pirate off his perch. Gideon is spilled from his hammock. The dim oil-lamp falls by his feet, and fear of fire has him snuff it out, leaving a darkness thick as pitch. They hear, but do not see, poor Scoresby slide the length of the cabin to crash into the door, with a muffled yelp. Only Zannah's grip prevents her being tossed from her berth on top of him. 'She's broached!' she yells.

Never before had they known their ship be pushed

right on to her side by wind and wave, and neither knows what will happen next. They stare at the patch of darkness that holds each other's anxious breathing. 'She'll right,' gasps Gideon, wincing at the bruises the ship's ribs have given his own. 'She must.'

The shouts outside are louder and more urgent now, but the moan in the rigging has died, if only because half the rigging, and the reefed-down sails, now trail in the heaving sea.

They wait. If their ship, their home, is to right herself, it has to be now. She'd not last long, broached-to, in seas like this. Zannah reaches down to comfort Scoresby, and through him, herself. Her stroking palm finds his hammering heart. She counts. After ten dog heartbeats she's sure the ship's not rolling any further. At twenty-five a shudder courses through all the timbers of their struggling vessel, as she begins to come upright. Tons of water spill down from the sails, thundering on to the thin planking overhead, and the moan starts up in the rigging again, this time topped by the furious flogging of the remaining unrestrained canvas.

'Fifty,' calls Zannah. 'We're all right.'

Gideon's not sure – *fifty what?* he thinks – not until he can see again the cloud-scudded moon through the porthole by his head. By its weak light he finds and relights the oil-lamp, with a trembling hand. Zannah tends to Scoresby, lifting him into the hammock she's just vacated, while Gideon tries to catch Pirate, who flutters round the tiny cabin, convinced that only the air is now safe. When he's calmed the bird, Zannah hands him his sea-boots. Her own are already on, and she's slipping into an oilskin.

'They won't want us out there,' says Gideon, even as he pulls the boots on.

'I know. But that's why we must go. We'll clean up in here later.'

The deck is more orderly than they've any right to expect in such a gale, there being nothing loose to be flung about, but aloft there rages a turmoil that dwarfs the chaos of their cabin. Unsheeted sails crack angrily in the keening wind, and the ropes that should control them whip around the rigging like furious snakes, striking at the foot-rope figures who struggle to rein them in. At least one yard is broken, and hangs at an awkward angle like a broken limb.

Joshua is everywhere on deck, pointing, calling orders, working the ropes, urging on his crew. He's stunned to find his twins among them, but any relief at seeing them safe is soon chased away. 'Below!' he insists. 'This is no place for you.'

'But we want to help' Zannah pleads, turning to Simva as she rushes up.

Simva lifts Gideon's hood. Only then does Zannah see, and Gideon feel, the sticky blood that oozes down his cheek. The pain in his ribs that still stifles his breathing has masked all awareness of the crack on the head he took at the same time.

Simva wipes the worst of the blood away and turns to Joshua. 'Below has its hazards too, Joshua. At least up here we can watch them.'

Joshua ponders a moment, eyeing the two men who struggle with the helmwheel. 'Aye,' he relents. 'Two are not enough on the helm, yet we can spare no more.' He bends to his children, and ties a short but stout rope around each waist. 'One on each side, in front of the men already there. Do *exactly* what they say. And tie yourselves on. Understand?'

Zannah and Gideon nod agreement as Simva leads them to the wheel, where she ties them to the stanchions nearby. Gideon lines up in front of Vincent, and Zannah in front of Nathan. The men give them the briefest of smiles then stare ahead, through eyes red-rimmed by salt water spray.

Gideon grasps a spoke of the huge wheel, and immediately feels an unfamiliar vibration in the massive rudder it controls. A black boiling wave lifts the stern of the ship, slewing her bows round to starboard, and rolling her hard. 'Down, lad!' shouts Vincent, and together they pull the helm hard over. Gideon's feet leave the deck for a moment, before the ship straightens up and Vincent calls again: 'Easy there.'

Now the same wave lifts the bows, slewing them back to port, and rolling her the other way. Gideon hears Nathan call to his sister on the other side of the wheel, and feels their effort in the wood. When Nathan calls 'Easy,' Gideon glances across to his sister, and sees the tight concentration in her face. They smile at each other, briefly, nervously, but are soon back at work: for it is the same with every wave surging across the ocean and under the *Unicorn*, one after another.

Soon Vincent and Nathan need shout no more, for the twins are quick learners, and have helmed before, if only in calmer times. After what Zannah guesses to be half an hour, but feels so much longer, her young muscles burn and cramp. The first grey hints of dawn tell her Nathan and Vincent have helmed almost a whole night watch, and in a full gale: and still they stand, strong and sharp and concentrated, absolutely alive and set on staying so. From the corner of her eye Zannah watches Vincent, standing tall behind her brother, and staring at the foam-flecked crests of the waves ahead. If he's weary he does not show it, and if cold he does not shiver. It's almost as if he's enjoying it.

He wipes his salt-streaked face and flashes her a quick smile, aware of her scrutiny. 'When you've sailed through a hurricane,' he tells her, ''tis hard to be daunted by lesser tempests.' She hesitates, then smiles back, before turning to face ahead again. *Whatever else he might be*, she thinks, *he's a sailor through and through, as much as Nathan beside him. And at times like these, every one on board depends on everyone else. We need him, as he needs us.*

Gideon's thoughts have wandered a different path. He asks himself if being allowed to help at the helm means he and and his sister have graduated as sailors; or if the ship really is in trouble. But at least things seem more ordered above: one by one the sails have been sheeted in, the ropes controlled, the broken yards cut away by the dim figures who crawl around the rigging like seabooted spiders.

As the light grows, the wind seems to ease, and the waves lose some of their violence. Rosa emerges from the galley, with mug after mug of hot thick soup. First Zannah and then Gideon are allowed to take their hands off the wheel for the few moments it takes to down the delicious warming broth. They smile salty thanks at Rosa, but when they return to the wheel, Rosa shakes her head. 'Strict orders. A mug of soup, and then below. You've done your part, and the worst is past.' Gideon hesitates, but Rosa is ready. 'And you have beasts to tend.'

Hot soup and a night of toil open yawns as wide as a hold-hatch. Zannah and Gideon do what they can to tidy their cabin. Pirate is asleep, or pretending to be, atop a pile of spilled peanuts or, rather, their shells, while Scoresby twitches in dreams of land-rabbits, and the unaccustomed luxury of a hammock berth. Zannah feels guilty at turfing him out, but fatigue beats any finer feeling at a time like this. She and Gideon are asleep before two swings of their hammocks: his side-to-side, hers fore-and-aft.

Around noon they are stirred by shifts in the sound and movement of the ship. Gideon has roused first, woken by the dull pain in his ribs, and the sharp sting of his cheek. He watches Zannah reach up to the same place on her own face, and then frown briefly before she remembers that it was he who was injured. 'Your ribs feel better though,' she says.

He nods, waiting for her to register the changes around them, as he did minutes before. The wind-shriek in the rigging has dwindled to a low hum. Waves no longer break over the bow to crash on to the deck, though they continue to lift and roll the ship. But the most striking absence is the bubbling rush of water along the hull planking: the *Unicorn* is no longer moving.

So many times have they experienced the dislocation of sleep in a ship on passage, that they think nothing of it. They have taken to bed on a starlit Pacific night, with no hint of land, and woken, swinging at anchor off a beach teeming with people, and pigs, and canoes; or turned in, amid driving harbour rain, and risen to find the decks already dry and the city far astern. But this is new. When they slumped, exhausted, into their hammocks at dawn the ship was still driving hard; but now, when the storm has passed, she is treading water.

Gideon sees the question in his sister's eyes. 'Yes,' he answers. 'We're hove to.'

And sure enough, when they emerge on deck, it is

74

to find their storm-battered vessel with her sails backed, and helm lashed hard over, so that she lies stationary in the water as the waves sweep under and past. She rides the swell so much more easily now, for she's no longer surging through the waves, crashing from crest to crest. It is much easier to move about – and to cook, as the smells from Rosa's galley attest – but heaving-to is rarely resorted to in mid-ocean: at the height of a storm too bad to sail through; to confer with another ship; or in an emergency.

There's an anxious conclave in the stern, with most of the crew bent over the taffrail, where two stout ropes have been tied, either side of the rudder, and now drop to the water.

'Surely not,' mutters Gideon, counting the ship's boats.

Zannah's doing the same. 'They're all there,' she says.

'It would be madness to lower boats in this swell,' says Gideon as they approach.

But no madness to launch men, it seems, for each rope bears a soaking sailor – Hal to port, Jacques to starboard. For seconds at a time they are buried in the swell, as it rises, but they are intent on something at the rudder vital enough to make them endure it.

Eventually Hal signals, and they are both heaved on board, spluttering and sodden. Jacques reaches for a blanket and shakes his head. He can hardly speak for shivers. 'Not g-g-good, I zink. N-N-Not good at all.'

An unaccustomed frown clouds Kanaka's face. 'But –'

Joshua looks to Hal.

'Looks like the p-p- pintles. Almost g-g-gone. M-m-musta cracked when we b-b-b-b-b-broached.'

Kanaka's frown deepens. 'But I checked, in Tahiti. I dived, as I always do before a long passage. I spent a day checking everything.'

There's an awkward silence till Nathan, who bears the blankets, speaks up. 'I'd say the crack *caused* the broach. We almost lost her completely. I was alone on the helm. If it hadn't been for Vincent, she'd never have come up. And ever after, all night, she was a demon to steer. Even with two –' he acknowledges the twins '– no, *four* of us.'

Joshua thinks aloud. 'If it goes altogether . . . We lose all steerage. Maybe the rudder falls off.'

'Ah d-d-don't zink it will last anuzer g-g-gale like las' night.'

'How far to Japan?' asks Simva.

'Too far.'

'And back to Sitka?'

'Further yet.'

'Then what option have we?'

'North,' says Vincent. He's been so quiet that he startles Zannah beside him. 'The Aleutians. Two days, at the most. And the wind is already taking us there.'

'You know the islands?' Simva's surprised. No Westerners go there: they've no cause to.

'Somewhat.'

'And what is there for us on those rocks?' This – even more startling – from the always quiet Sven, and addressed more to Joshua than Vincent.

Joshua lets Vincent answer. 'A harbour for repairs and some room for trade.'

Sven scowls. 'Trade? Trade *what?*'

Joshua whispers to Zannah to bring up on deck the topmost chart from the table in his cabin below. Sven's so worked up he doesn't see her go, but he doesn't have the words to vent his rage. He clenches and unclenches his hands.

Zannah's soon back to hand over the chart, but Joshua takes his time, smoothing the creased parchment over the hatch cover. His crew crowd round as his finger lights on the pencilled X he marked an hour before, the latest in a line of Xs stretching westwards over the vast North Pacific, from one speckled coastal sleeve to another. 'Our noon position. Here's Sitka. Here's Japan.'

It seems so far in either direction. But Zannah sees – they all see – that Vincent is right. For above the ocean, unnoticed and almost unknown, is strung a slender necklace of pearly dots of land, in a crescent a thousand miles long. The nearest is so close Zannah raises her eye to the horizon, wondering if she might see it. Gideon does the same.

Joshua looks up at the big Swede towering over him. 'Sven?'

And Sven speaks at last, with more words than anyone's heard him use in one go. 'First we give up Sitka. Now Japan. To swop rotting pelts and cheap vodka with Russian drunkards? Pah!'

Joshua answers quietly. 'If we try for Sitka or Japan, when our rudder hangs by a thread, we will give up a great deal more than money. It is not a chance I wish to take.' He looks Sven steadily in the eye. 'Would you have us vote on it?'

Sven glances around, then grunts and stomps off, back to brooding silence. Vincent's keen eyes watch him go, and follow him a little longer than anyone else's.

Joshua rolls up the chart. 'Then north it is. We will nurse that rudder like a new-born, and we will carry just enough sail to give us way.'

'Maybe we should take turns to breathe,' gasps Gideon, as he pretends to expire. He and his sister are crammed into the crow's nest. In southern waters there had always been room for them both, but now, swaddled as they are in layers of cold-weather clothing, their lofty barrel holds them in a tight woody embrace. They cannot turn to scan the horizon – the reason they're up here – so they've assigned quadrants of it, with an area of overlap marked out by the bowsprit's swinging arc.

Sven and Vincent work the wheel, while Kanaka and Nathan hammer away on deck, building a sturdy framework to clamp on to the vulnerable rudder. Joshua's below, studying charts, while Hal and Jacques dry themselves and their clothes by Rosa's galley stove. Simva's at the bowsprit, more eager than anyone for land. She knows that, despite Sven's rant about drunken Russians, these islands they seek are peopled by the Aleut, close cousins to her Inuit kin. For all the vast distance between here and her Greenland home, the Aleut speak much as she does. She waves to her twins high above.

They wave back. Vincent's told them what to look for: the plume of smoke from the mighty volcano named Shishaldin, on Unimak island. 'It should be to the North-East,' he'd said. 'That's what we'll see first.

There's other volcanos, but none as angry as Shishaldin. It smokes all the time.'

Gideon and Zannah take turns with the spyglass, to ease their aching eyes. There are clouds ahead, puffy and scudding, which merge and part, revealing gaps into which the spyglass must be poked in the search for smoke.

While Zannah has the glass, Gideon daydreams. He looks to the stern, where Vincent's engaged Sven more deeply in conversation than anyone else has managed since Tahiti. They fall silent when Joshua comes on deck to confer with Nathan, but Gideon doesn't register this.

Gideon's glad they'll see a volcano after all, even if it's not in Japan. *Ten thousand feet high*, Vincent said. Gideon hopes they'll let him climb it, and look inside, into the glowing heart of the world.

There's a dig in his ribs, then Zannah stands very still. 'I think I see it,' she whispers. Gideon's eager for the glass, but when she hands it over he has trouble finding the gap in the clouds. Zannah guides him till he sees it too: a distant snowy cone, silver in the sun, standing proudly above the horizon, and breathing a grey-white plume which stretches away in the wind. He lowers the glass, and marks the bearing, nodding at Zannah.

'Together?' she asks.

'Together!' he smiles, and they lean out of their barrel, shouting for all they are worth to their crew-mates below. 'Land Ho! Laaand Ho!'

Simva's soon up beside them, as excited as they are. Gideon hands her the glass, as she hangs in the rigging, and she sees it too, just as the cloud-gap closes. 'It's Shishaldin!' she shouts down. 'Four points to starboard!' Immediately Joshua goes below to busy himself with charts and instruments.

Simva brushes the cheek of each twin in turn. 'Well done, my little eagles.' She laughs to see them jammed in. 'Only not so little now, eh? You outgrow your nest, I think.' Zannah mimes the open gape of a hungry eagle chick. Gideon and Simva laugh.

'Do you recall your Inuit?' asks Simva. Gideon nods, but he knows he doesn't retain more than a few words, though his sister holds more in her head. Zannah looks to the North-East, to where the volcano lies. 'Does it have an Inuit – an Aleut – name?' she asks.

Simva follows her gaze. 'It does, only we don't know it, and of course it is not on the charts. These capes and mountains are given the names of Russian princes and American senators who will never see them. There is even an English Bay, named for Captain Cook.'

'He sailed here?' asks Zannah.

81

'He sailed *everywhere*,' says Gideon, with pride. 'But he started in Whitby, just like this ship.'

'And just like her captain.' Simva cannot help sharing a little of his pride, but she also knows what Whitby whalers, and others like them, had brought her people, and others like *them*.

'Shishaldin is a Russian name, and a recent one. The Aleut are people of the sea and have no time for mountains: but they will use that volcano to navigate by, as we do now, so they will have a name for it.' She hands back the spyglass. 'It will have had that name for centuries.' Just before she drops back down to the deck, she fixes Gideon with a steady look. 'One of your jobs, Giddy, when we land, is to find out what it is, so you can amend the chart. Give the mountain its name back.'

The crew as a whole are now so intent on the cloud-gaps ahead, and the teasing glimpses of Unimak and the other islands, that none of them bar Joshua look astern, and when he calls for more sail it comes as a surprise. They turn and see what he's been watching a while now: an angry bank of storm cloud, growling over the southern horizon, and racing North, and with no gaps in it at all.

'I fear we find ourselves in a race,' Joshua tells the helmsmen. 'Will we make the land before that tempest is upon us?'

It soon seems the answer is no. They lay on sail after sail, to try and speed their progress, fragile rudder or not. When he feels the first puffs of the rising wind, and the clouds blot out the sinking sun, Joshua reverses his orders, and the same sails are all speedily furled again. Immediately after the twins have spotted the island they're looking for, off to the west of Shishaldin, Joshua calls them down from their perch to the deck, where they join the general efforts to lash and stow every moveable object, dog and parrot included.

By the time the storm hits there is minimal canvas aloft, everything is secured, and lifelines are rigged the length of the deck. Everyone is fully kitted out in oilskins and seaboots, and Rosa's distributed the last hot food they might see for a while. As they eat quickly in shifts, Joshua explains that the only anchorage marked on the charts lies on the far side of the island, round a prominent headland. Once there they'll be sheltered and safe. Barely has he uttered these words than the wind, as if affronted, falls upon them, and the rigging's a-shriek again.

There are two crew on each side of the helm, and two

more standing by, but working the wheel is harder and harder, so the ship wallows and corkscrews in the rapidly steepening waves. Zannah's not been seasick for years, but the feeling's there now, and a clammy knot tightens where her stomach should be, try though she may not to let it show. Simva ushers her and Gideon into the galley, shouting to Rosa over the roar of wind and spray, to watch them well, before she returns to her post by the compass.

Joshua watches the compass needle swing wildly as the ship yaws over each wave. 'It's no good,' he shouts to Nathan, at the helm. 'We're being driven too far west. Will she point up at all?'

Nathan tries, but a grinding creak from the rudder is heard by all, above the fury of the storm, as soon as he pulls the helm over. It's clear now they have little choice about where they go.

The crack is even heard in the galley, where Gideon looks across the table to Zannah. The same thoughts run past them both: *a rising storm . . . a lee shore, unmarked, uncharted, unknown . . . night coming on . . . and the steering as good as gone.* But neither gives them voice.

Gideon sees the sweaty pallor in his sister's face, and wonders how soon he'll feel the same way. He scratches his memory for words. Inuit words. Eventually one comes to the surface, and he taps the side of his nose. 'Angusix,' he says.

At first Zannah's too preoccupied with her own stomach to think about anyone else's nose, but when he repeats it she understands. Angusix – nose. She sticks out her tongue. 'Agnax!' she says.

Gideon laughs. 'I thought for a minute you were going to be sick on me!'

'Never!' declares Zannah. 'I know the word but I'll never –'

'Let's not even think it,' Gideon butts in, as he too grows pale.

The table between them is bucking ever more violently, and the pots and pans jangle angrily against each other. It's getting hard to hold on. A wave breaks over the deck, and a wall of water slams against the galley walls.

Zannah's eyes are open wide, so Gideon leans forward, staring like an owl, and blinking exaggeratedly, till their foreheads almost touch. 'Datuu. Eyes,' he hums.

Zannah's hand stretches over the table towards his, where he holds on, knuckles ever whiter. She clasps it and says, 'Chakin. Hands.'

'What do you mean?' demands Gideon. 'My hands aren't shaking at all!'

A porthole shatters as another wave strikes, and they are showered with broken glass and freezing sea-water. Rosa's struck by a flying pan, and falls to the floor. The door bursts open, but it is Joshua, and not the sea, that crashes in. Behind him, by the wheel, Vincent indicates to the struggling helmsmen with shouts and gestures of command, like a second captain. It's almost dark.

'Get on the floor!' Joshua shouts. 'Under that table, and hold on as best you can.'

Zannah rolls Rosa under the table, as Gideon pulls her from the other side, then they squeeze underneath themselves.

Joshua crouches low to make himself heard. 'We cannot make the anchorage, and have no choice but to run her up the beach. It will be bumpy.' And he's gone, like a receding wave.

Through the swinging door and amid lashing rain the twins glimpse Simva, Joshua and the crew fighting with the helmwheel. Framed in the portholes are towering hills close by on either side: they're speeding through a narrow channel, running into a bay. Rosa's pain is heard in the grinding of her teeth, though she does not cry out. 'Is it bad?' asks Zannah.

Rosa turns to her and forces a smile. She holds up the pan. 'I don't think it's broken. We'll have broth from it yet, my child, once we are ashore.'

Gideon shifts to let Rosa lie straighter, and speaks to them both. 'Father told me a story about this once. In Whitby. A ship with its steering gone ran up the beach in a storm. A big dog jumped off the bows.' He turns to Zannah. 'Everyone survived. This is a Whitby ship. She's built for it.'

There's a shout at the wheel, as the whole crew wrenches it hard to port, then another, louder shout, and they dive to the deck, scrambling for the lifelines.

'This is it!' says Gideon. He decides not to close his eyes. Zannah too.

And then the ship strikes, in a juddering crash which goes on and on and on. Timbers groan and splinter below deck, while aloft the foremast collapses with a terrible rending. Bodies tumble about the deck like scattered skittles, bumping against the woodwork. Hal is hurled through the door into the galley, where he sprawls across the twins' feet.

Zannah waits for who-knows-how-many heartbeats till the ship comes finally to a halt, groaning in woody pain, and still pounded by unforgiving surf. At least now the deck is no longer heaving, and one by one they pick themselves up, bruised and wincing, to answer Simva's head count.

As soon as he's sure all have escaped serious harm, Joshua's up at the bowsprit. He can see the beach, but between the safety it offers and the shattered ship lies a hundred yards of boiling surf.

'We'll never swim that,' says Nathan.

'And she'll break up under this pounding,' Joshua replies, as another shudder runs through the timbers underfoot. 'We must get a line ashore.'

'There's the cannon,' cries Nathan, and in a moment he and Kanaka, who's managed to light an oil-lamp, are rummaging in the chaos of the fo'c's'le to unbury a tiny, toy-like cannon, stowed there years before and barely used since. Emerging from its muzzle, like a hermit crab from its shell, is a grappling hook, attached by a long light line.

Joshua peers in. 'Have we powder?'

Nathan waves the small cask he's slipped from the muzzle. 'Aye, and it may yet be dry.' He works quickly to load the cannon, to stuff the grappling hook in place, and to smooth out the coils of line and make sure they'll run free. Kanaka hands him a length of fuse which he puts in place, and they look to their captain for a signal.

Joshua's peering into the night, not at the beach, but at the deeper darkness of the rocks beside it, where there's a chance the hook will find a hold. He turns to

Nathan. 'We'll only get one shot, I think.' Kanaka lights a taper from his oil-lamp. Together he and Nathan carry the cannon on to the fore-deck, to the point Joshua indicates. They lower it quickly, and as the fuse is lit, Hal jams a piece of broken yard-arm behind the cannon to take its recoil. Jacques stands over the fizzing fuse with his opened oilskins spread wide, to shelter it from the driving spray. He coughs in the smoke, looking to Zannah like some devilish dwarf bent over a hellish smithy.

There's a huge flash, and a bigger bang, and they're thrown backwards, momentarily blinded and unable to see where the hook has gone. Joshua reels the line in, and tugs it hard. 'Seems fast,' he shouts, as he ties it to a stanchion. He picks up a heavier rope and ties it round his waist, then swings over the rail. Surf surges far below his feet.

'Must you go?' pleads Simva. Joshua looks at her, holding her in his gaze a moment before he speaks. 'I'll not ask anyone else to do it,' he says, as softly as the storm allows. He indicates the rope round his waist. 'When I've taken this line ashore, everyone is to follow along it. Bring such other lines you can, and get the essentials ready on deck. We may not have long.'

And with that he clambers down, using the tangled

rigging of the collapsed foremast as a ladder, till the waves are breaking up to his waist. He steps off the rigging, entrusting himself, his family, his crew to the slender grappling line he grips in his battered hands. It gives.

He is hurled into the sea, swept under, and smashed by wave after wave, every time he surfaces. His crew frantically haul in his waist-rope. When they pull him up he is vomiting seawater, and blue with cold and bruises and lack of air; but he's alive and he's conscious. 'Too heavy,' he gasps as he sprawls on the deck.

Nathan shouts back that the hook has caught again, and immediately Vincent's in motion, stripping off seaboots and oilskins. 'I'm lighter,' he says. 'I'll go.'

But he's not quick enough. 'Remember the dog?' Zannah asks Gideon. 'The Whitby dog?' She gives him a rope and ties one end round her waist. 'I'm lightest of all. I'm going off the bowsprit.' She thrusts a harpoon into his hands. 'You'll have to hold them off, with this, Giddy, long enough to let me. Let's go!'

Before Vincent can take it up Zannah dashes forward and snatches the grappling line from his hands. She springs to the bowsprit and scrambles along it, trying not to hear the shouting behind her. Gideon follows close after, but at the base of the bowsprit whirls round and swishes the harpoon at his pursuers.

First among them is his mother. 'Zannah! No!' she screams, as her daughter vanishes in the spray and the murk of the night: but her way is blocked by Gideon and his harpoon, which he swings repeatedly, waiting for his sister to tell him she has gone.

Zannah hesitates at the very end of the bowsprit, glad that the darkness prevents her seeing the worst of the seething sea below. She coils the grappling line loosely in one hand, shouts to Giddy, takes a deep breath, and jumps.

Drenched and frozen though she already is, the shocking cold of the water clutches at her chest like a vice. She wills herself to hold on to her breath till she surfaces, if only she could tell where the surface is. She is rolled and tumbled and somersaulted by the waves, till she cannot tell up from down or air from water. When she is briefly, and painfully, pounded against gravel, she knows she has a chance. She pushes down hard with her legs, finds something solid, and springs up far enough to refill her desperate lungs. Immediately she's immersed again, but now she's hauling hard on the grappling line. There's much more slack than she remembers leaving, and she prays that the hook still holds.

Back on board, Gideon hurls his harpoon aside. He's

done what she asked, and done it instinctively, and known it was right. He would have asked it of her, if she'd not beaten him to it. But he's just swung a harpoon at all the people he's ever loved; and his twin, his half-self, has vanished beneath the surface and left no sign.

The salt in his eyes is not just spray when, after an age, a shout goes up. He blinks his tears away to see, dimly but definitely, a tiny figure rise above the water for an instant, pulling herself through the foam hand over hand along the grappling line. And now he shouts too, louder than anyone. 'Go Zannah! Go Zannah! Go Zannah!'

She hears his shouts above the tumult and they wring from her muscles her dwindling reserves of strength. She's almost ashore, but each wave smashes the breath out of her, and batters her with gravel, till her grip has nearly gone.

She's also watched from shore. Hiding from view, and the storm, is a crouching huddle of people, anxiously questioning each other about this stricken ship and who it might bring among them. 'Promyshleniki?' is the word on all their lips, till the tallest among them stands up. He sees Zannah clearly for the first time, as she finally loses her grip and falls backward, exhausted, into the water, to the sound of screams from the ship.

He races forward, wading forcefully into the surf to grab her limp body and bring her ashore. As he lays her on the gravel his companions approach and bend over her, astonished to see that she shares with them their dark hair, dark skin, black eyes, high cheekbones. The tall one unties her waist-rope, and makes it fast to a huge boulder at the head of the beach.

Before he has finished his knot Simva's over the gunwale, hauling herself furiously along the line to the security of land. She bends to her daughter, and then, hearing her gasp, and seeing her open her eyes, embraces the tall man, and lets loose a torrent of grateful Inuit and ecstatic tears.

The rest of the crew are quickly ashore, bringing more lines, and the essentials Joshua spoke of: sextant, charts, compass, hunting knives, a gun, and more. Joshua is last to join them, bearing Gideon on his back. In front of him Hal hauls a whimpering Scoresby, slung round his shoulders like so much meat. Somewhere in the darkness a battered bird-cage with a petrified parrot is hauled along a rough rope to land.

Joshua lowers Gideon to the beach, where Simva hands him Scoresby's lead, and guides him away, up to the grassy hummocks above the gravel. At the top of the beach she turns, to see her husband, still ankle deep in surf, and so intent on watching his tortured ship that he scarcely notices her return to his side.

'Come, Joshua,' she says, as she takes his arm. 'We must shelter.' But he doesn't move, just gazes out to sea, at the fearful pounding the *Unicorn* is taking. Now that he and his ship are parted, he seems dazed, only half-aware of anything else.

Slowly he turns to face Simva, and gestures at the violence of the waves as they crash over the *Unicorn*. 'What am I without my ship? Who am I if not her captain?' The battle being fought in the bay nearly drowns his words. He raises his voice to be sure he is heard, and points at the shuddering masts. 'Where is my home, if not on the deck of that ship, at sea?'

Simva leads him up the beach, and when she feels the tussocky grass underfoot she speaks, to break his trance. 'We can do nothing about her now. The sea will have her or it will not. And with her or without her, you are still our captain, and husband and father, and your home is with us, wherever we are. Perhaps even here.'

He looks about. 'You spoke of shelter. Where is it?' Only then does he notice that none of his crew are to be seen, though he was sure they'd all reached shore. He frowns.

Simva indicates with her foot. 'You're standing on it.' And with that, a light flickers from an opening in the ground to his left, and smoke streams from another to his right. He hears coughing and low talk from both, and he turns to Simva, aware now that though his ship may be fighting for her life, his wife, their twins, and the crew are all safe.

CHAPTER 4
THE CALLING IN THE FOG

GIDEON'S SHIVERS EASE AS HE WRAPS THE strange fur tightly around his shoulders. He looks about, in the flickering light cast by a pair of oil-lamps and the single fire, still smoky-young. He, his family, and his crew sit, or slump, in an oval house set into the ground. There is a single large central room, with an opening in the roof above the fire. Gusts of wind blow smoke back down, to add to the sporadic coughs, and to soften the light. On either side low alcoves open off the main room, with bare frames that may once have been beds for small people. At the far end, away from the light, is another opening, through which a notched log ascends as a ladder from the shadows within to the howling darkness without. Cobwebs cling to Gideon's face when he peers into the nearest alcove, and puffs of dust rise from the floor when he shuffles back towards the fire. It is the first time he has felt land underfoot since a hot Tahitian beach, now thousands of miles to the south.

Dim blanketed shipmate-shadows huddle around the fire, while other figures – smaller, darker, and garbed in furs like his own – flit between them, offering drinks, morsels of food, and words of comfort in a language both oddly familiar and strangely new. Before the fire, two of the strangers flank Simva, and, with her, bend low over Zannah, who twitches and coughs in a troubled half-sleep.

One stranger mutters to Simva, who answers in the same guttural language, and nods. A small stone bottle is produced from under a cloak, a tight-fitting stopper is prised out, and three or four drops of syrupy liquid are poured on to Zannah's tongue. She coughs again, but only once, then settles. Simva smiles down at her, then at the strangers by each shoulder. She looks around for Gideon, and beckons him closer.

His shivers are gone when he steps up to the inner circle of fire light. He looks down at his sleeping sister. 'Will she be all right?'

The strangers, who, with their broad high cheek-bones, red-brown skin, and black-black hair, look much like his mother, glance from Gideon to Zannah, then back to Gideon, and whisper to each other as Simva speaks. 'Yes. As will we all, for we have found shelter . . . and help.'

'Who are they?'

'They are the Aleut, and cousins to my – to *our* – people, the Inuit.'

There are footsteps on the ladder, and then on the floor, as someone enters and approaches.

Simva gestures at the space around her. 'This island is their home, and this hut – a *barbera*, they call it – was once one of their houses. It is now our shelter.'

'For the present, perhaps.' The footsteps halt. Gideon turns to see Joshua, dripping with rain and spray, and pinched with cold, returning from his third trip to the water's edge that night. He raises mottled blue hands to the warmth of the fire, and musters a smile for his wife and his son. 'The tempest eases.'

Gideon wakes at the stirring of the anchor-heavy weight on his feet. He stares about, disorientated and panicky for a moment, till his sea-dreams fall away, as sediment drops out of murky water, to leave it clear. The tickling at his nose is not seaweed fronds but fur. He lies in an alcove, now cobweb-free, not a submerged cave: and while the chalk-white beam overhead is indeed a whale bone, it supports the ceiling of a human home and not the belly of a living whale.

The lumpy mass that pins his feet is Scoresby, come to give and to get such comfort as he can. Gideon reaches down and strokes a velvet sleeping ear, while he looks around, more calmly now. The alcove is still in shadow, but shafts of chilly daylight pierce the ceiling of the main room, where the fire glows red under steaming breakfast pots. Zannah still lies nearby under a pile of furs, topped by an unhappy parrot. Her eyes flicker open briefly, meet his, and close again, narrowed a little by a faint smile.

The barbera is mostly empty of the ship's company who crowded within it last night, and entirely empty of Aleut. Gideon slips his legs from underneath his dog, enrobes himself in furs, and approaches his mother, who sits by Zannah and stirs the pot.

'Good afternoon,' she chides. Gideon can tell from her weary smile that she's sat up all night.

'So it wasn't a dream?'

'No. Sadly not. But the dreams which had you cry out so must have been worse. I had to send Scoresby over to quiet you.' At the mention of his name the dog lifts his head: but only briefly, when he sees there is no food yet.

'I dreamt he was an anchor, dragging me down to . . . to . . . what do they call it? Deep six? Full fathom five? Davy Jones?'

'Hush. They call it all of those things, but none apply to us, for we are all safe and sound and on dry land. Thanks to your sister.' Her hand runs idly through Zannah's glossy hair, then rises to grip Gideon's shoulder. 'And to you.' She fixes him with a questioning stare. 'But tell me . . . That harpoon – would you have used it?'

Gideon squirms and looks away. 'I did use it. All I needed was to give her time to go.'

'And oh how she went.' Anger suddenly clouds Simva's face, like a tropical squall. 'Now listen, Gideon. We owe you a great deal, but if you or your sister ever *ever* do anything like that again, I'll – I'll –'

Zannah rescues him with a cough. Simva turns aside, the anger-cloud already gone.

Gideon seizes his chance. 'Where's Father?'

'Out with the crew, surveying the ship. They've been up since first light.'

'The ship? Then she's not sunk?'

'Quite the opposite. There's barely a foot of water under her bows. She's beached, and broken, Giddy, like a stranded whale.'

And he's gone, racing up the ladder into the light, trailing his furry cape behind, and oblivious to his mother's entreaties to eat.

Outside, Gideon steps off the ladder, facing north, away from the sea and the sudden dazzle of the sun, and waits while his eyes adapt. Underfoot, the turfed roof of the barbera merges with the thick grass of the slopes, which trend away, treeless and fox-brown, to the snowline and the cloud-clad hills. Dead ahead is a kind of pass, marking, he guesses, a stream's valley, still snowbound, but not so thickly as the peaks on either side.

Gideon turns to face south, and squints into the low sun, its glare undimmed in a gunmetal sky. The stillness is total: not a blade of grass stirs, and the smoke from the fire below rises languidly but directly upwards, mocking memories of last night's storm.

The grassy slope drops away to a shingle beach, which runs off in a tight curve on either side, to end in a scattering of rocks, two of which stand like gate-posts, enclosing the bay. Gideon peers at the gap between them and his heart skips a beat: a few feet to port, or a yard or two to starboard, and they would have been pulverised.

Where last night the water had surged right over the beach and on to the slopes, today it barely enters the bay, exposing a broad sweep of seaweed, sand, bird-pocked mud, and barnacled rocks. And here, thrown on to her side, with a tangle of spars and rigging trailing into the water, is the *Unicorn*.

Curious Aleut look on as Joshua and the rest of the crew wade slowly and silently around her, in water no more than knee-deep. Gideon sets off, wanting to run, but his legs offer no more than a leaden walk, as if at a funeral.

At the water's edge Gideon waits and watches for a long time, as the quiet figures circle the stricken vessel. This ship has been so many things to him: his birthplace, his unfailing shelter, his schoolroom and his playground. She has shown him so much: flying fish and phosphorescence; spinner dolphins in their hundreds; St Elmo's fire on the yard arm. She's brought him the deep joy of a moonlit Pacific lagoon, and the terror of a full Atlantic storm: and she's taught him how to handle both. She is the only home he's ever known, and here she lies, bleeding woody splinters into the rock-pools about her, while his father and the crew tend her, as nurses to a battle-stricken giant.

Joshua runs his hand along the line of a seam

between two planks, his head held against the curve of the hull. He raps on the planks with his knuckles, then drops to his knees and repeats this at the next plank down. Kanaka's doing the same at the bow. The Aleut watch, bemused, as if this is some ritual to bring the great wounded vessel back to life.

Gideon speaks at last. 'Where's it gone?'

Joshua's been concentrating so hard he hasn't noticed Gideon approach. The exposed reefs of heartbreak and loss Gideon glimpsed in him last night are already being covered by a rising tide of hope and determination. 'Gone?' He smiles wearily and wades further astern towards the rudder. Splinters swirl past his splashing thighs.

Gideon stays up the beach, careful to remain dry-shod. 'The water. It was twelve feet deep here last night.'

'And more. And there lies our great good fortune. We came in at the top of the tide, with a storm surge, and the barometer lower than I have seen it for years. Anything less and we'd have been dashed on the rocks for sure. But make no mistake, the water will be back, and may claim her yet.'

Nathan is cutting away the knotted rigging. "Twas more than fortune, son. No mere luck could bring us through yon narrow channel as Vincent and your father did. I'd swear they were born here.'

At the mention of his name, Vincent's head appears over the rail high above, where he and Hal have clambered aboard to the steeply canted deck. 'Not born here, Nathan. Just of a mind not to die here.' He hurls a length of shattered spar overboard. 'And how can you speak so of fortune to a man who has been shipwrecked twice since last he stood on dry land?'

Joshua raps again on the planking and shouts. It is the loudest noise all morning, and startles all about. 'How is she within?'

Jacques' muffled voice shouts back through the planking. 'Zere is water, bien sur, but not so much? I zink she is not 'oled.' There is a general release of breath among the ship's company, and a subtle but definite change in the set of their shoulders. The same thought runs through all heads: *We might save her still.*

Hal laughs. 'He sounds even Frencher through three inches of mahogany.'

Vincent calls down to Joshua. 'She's strong. Where was she built?'

Joshua pats the planking by his head and looks up, with a proud smile. 'Whitby. My father helped build her, like they built them all: strong enough to sit on the shore with a cargo of coal. Captain Cook took Whitby cats like these around the world. She's of that breed.' He runs his hand along the curving timber, as if caressing it, then lowers his brow to touch his ship's side, and his voice to address her. 'Good old girl,' he whispers. 'Good old girl.'

Gideon stands off still, so he can't be certain: but he'll tell Zannah later that he saw his father close his eyes and kiss the rough timbers, with a tenderness normally reserved for Simva or him and his sister – and then only rarely. He won't tell Zannah, for he can't be sure, that his father's eyes were a-glitter, and his voice stilled completely, while he embraced the stricken vessel he thought was gone for ever.

But Joshua's only quiet for a moment. He turns to Kanaka. 'And what of the bow?'

Kanaka's on hands and knees in the chilly water, feeling along the gouges and grazes where the ship had grounded. 'Some plank part sprung,' he calls back. 'Tree, maybe four. Notting too bad.'

There's a sucking noise as Hal sets to work with the bilge bump. After several strokes a splatter of water drops to the deck, across to the scuppers, and down the port side.

Joshua steps back to shallower water and gestures to Nathan. 'I reckon we can patch her up and refloat her, even if it's with only the one mast. What do you say?'

Nathan straightens his stiffening back and looks around at the barren hills. 'We've not much wood, and there's little enough growing here.' He runs his eye over the ship, from battered bow to skewed stern. 'It's a lot of work.' He meets Joshua's steady gaze, stretches out a pause, then gives the faintest flicker of a smile. 'But we've nothing else to do, eh? Not round here. So I say yes.'

'In two weeks? Before the next spring tides?'

'We'll need all hands. And maybe some of theirs.' Nathan indicates the Aleut. 'And we'll need to work every hour of daylight.'

Gideon breaks in. 'All hands? When do I start?'

Nathan hands him the rigging knife, and picks up a saw. 'Now.'

Zannah's obvious boredom tells Simva she's recovered, so when she asks, for the fifth time, to be allowed outside, Simva relents, and tells her she'll be along soon after.

Zannah traces her brother's steps up the ladder and into the light, but is greeted by a different sight than met him, for the crew are in animated action, working around and upon and inside the ship with an urgency that draws Zannah on in a run.

She spots Gideon at the dry end of a human chain, along which is passing everything moveable from the hold to the shore. Already there are piles of cargo and stores above the beach, over which Rosa lashes heavy tarpaulins. Zannah joins the chain next to Gideon. He winces when he takes a large box from Hal, and staggers as he turns to pass it to his sister. She braces her legs and back to take the weight, but when he drops it into her grasp she finds it so light it must surely be empty.

Gideon laughs. 'Feathers. Tropic bird feathers. Remember them?'

She does. She and her brother delighted in collecting these gaudy ornaments in Tahiti, and Hawaii, and Guinea, and in supplementing their finds with Pirate's cast-offs. When Joshua first mentioned Sitka, Simva knew at once the rich traders there would pay well for hat decorations such as these, and she promised the twins a share of the profit. Zannah carries the box up the beach to the spot where Rosa bids her begin a new pile. Little had she thought, when she packed it, that she'd later unload it on a barren beach in Alaska.

It's not long before they are shifting heavier items, requiring two or three or four people at a time to manhandle them ashore. Joshua rigs a ramp from the deep recesses of the hold to the lower edge of the canted hatch, and Nathan improvises a rope-and-pulley crane from the stump of the foremast, a broken spar, and the collapsed rigging. He lowers box after box into the eager hands of his crew-mates, who splash in water now well above their knees. They all know, though none of them says, that the tide is coming in.

Joshua emerges from the hold and calls down. 'Time's too tight to move it all. But we've taken enough to get at the ballast. If we shift that we can get at the sprung planks, and lighten her enough to get her further up the beach.'

Everyone climbs aboard, and most drop down into the hold, but Joshua calls his twins back. 'I don't want you down there with the heavy work. I want you to lay out the longest strongest ropes you can find in the fo'c's'le. We're going to haul her up the beach.'

Gideon and Zannah clamber forward, trying not to see the damage all around them. Behind them, Sven's already dragging a huge boulder up the ramp. He hurls it off the edge, and into the sea. Before the splash has subsided Hal and Jacques follow, hauling a similar rock between them. This ballast has been with them so long no one knows where it's from. Its sturdy weight, low down near the keel, has given the ship the stability that's allowed her to weather all the storms she's faced. All but one.

'Anyone seen Vincent?' Joshua shouts, to a general

shaking of heads, before he too descends for a boulder of his own.

Zannah indicates the Aleut, still looking on impassively from the shore. 'Will they not help?'

'Did they not help enough last night?' Gideon replies, as he opens up the fo'c's'le. 'Vincent tried to talk to them, before you came, but they just shook their heads. They don't like being told what to do.'

'Hmmm.' Zannah frowns. 'Especially if it's him doing the telling, I'll bet.'

She joins him in poking around the tangled chaos of the fo'c's'le for stowed ropes, pulling out a loose end here, a loop there, while Gideon clears the debris as best he can.

'You still don't like him?' he asks. 'How many times must he save us before you'll admit you were wrong?'

'There's something I . . . I just . . . I don't . . .' Her voice trails away, and a silence hangs in the air between them, till she reaches forward, then stands with the end of a stout hemp line hanging from her hand. 'Here. This is one of them.'

She takes it up on to the foredeck, coiling it carefully as Gideon frees the rest of it from the mess and passes it up to her, six feet at a time. The grunts and splashes at the hatch continue, but are suddenly stilled when they all feel a lurch underfoot. Nathan points out the quiver in the mast. 'She's startin' to rise,' he calls, over the loudening ripple of returning tide.

Joshua bids Kanaka join him at the bow, where they take Zannah's line, pass it through the starboard anchor hawse, and let the end drop into the water. Joshua scrambles over the rail and down to the water, then drags the rope up the beach, fashions a large bowline, and drops it over an outcrop of rock. He does the same on the port side, with another length of line, then rejoins Hal on deck. They wrap the lines round the capstan drum, and haul in the slack, till the ropes are tight and groaning.

Gideon and Zannah join them, straining against the capstan bars on the sloping jumble of the deck: but nothing happens. 'Not yet,' says Joshua. 'We need more water and less ballast still.'

All bar the twins are down in the hold or on the ramp now, so when the next, bigger lurch comes, they all hear the cannon crack of breaking plank, and the rush of incoming water from the bows.

'To the pumps!' Joshua shouts up to Gideon and Zannah: and in an instant they are at the heavy brass handles either side of the mainmast. The *Unicorn* was normally so watertight she rarely needed pumping, but they know what to do nonetheless, and they set to with gusto, working to pump the water out at least as fast as it gushes in below.

Zannah pushes her handle down while Gideon's rises, using her weight rather than her muscles, as she has been shown. Even so it is hard work, and as they see-saw either side of the mast, they struggle to find a rhythm that works.

'Let's sing,' Zannah puffs.

Gideon shakes his head. 'No breath,' he pants, on the upstroke. When he applies his weight to his handle he grunts, a sound spelling urgency and effort.

The water they raise spills over the deck, then into the scuppers and back into the sea. There's a sound like a distant gunshot, and another lurch, the biggest yet, as the deck comes almost level.

Gideon finds breath enough to speak. 'If she's rising . . . we must be winning.'

Zannah nods. 'I think . . . we've pumped . . . the same bit of water . . . three times already.'

Gideon and Zannah redouble their work at the handles, while Joshua, Nathan, Hal and the rest set to at the capstan, with a 'Yo Heave Ho!' This, and the creak of the ropes, tell of their effort, but still the ship will not budge.

'You need skids!' There's a voice on the beach: Vincent's voice. He stands with a rifle slung across his shoulder, and a dead seal on the stones at his feet. Simva draws up behind him dragging a bundle of driftwood logs.

'So it *was* a gunshot,' Zannah hisses at her brother.

As they work, the twins watch Vincent set about the seal carcass with his knife, while Simva places the logs before the *Unicorn*, like a wooden staircase rising up the beach. Vincent smears seal-fat and blubber over the first two logs, and kicks them hard under the ship's bows.

Another yo-heave-ho yields movement, but only a matter of inches. Gideon and Zannah quit the pump to join their crew-mates at the capstan bars, but to no avail. 'She's still stuck!' Nathan calls.

Harsh shouts from the beach rise above the grunts and laboured breathing at the capstan. Over her shoulder Zannah sees Vincent gesticulating at the Aleut. His bloody knife points at the seal's carcass, his rifle's slipped off his shoulder, and his face contorts as he yells at them in something near their own language.

The Aleut get up slowly and approach the ship. Only then does Zannah see her mother, who is also addressing the Aleut but quietly, pleadingly. She moves to stand between them and Vincent, but still they watch him warily as they pass by.

With the Aleut and Simva adding to the effort at the capstan bars, and Vincent working the seal-greased skids, the ship moves again, to a sudden roar: 'Now, lads! Keep her moving now! All your strength!'

And keep her moving they do. Amid shouting, and tumbling round the capstan, and furious work by Vincent right under her bows, the *Unicorn* makes her stately progress up the beach, inch by inch, foot by foot, till at last Joshua is satisfied and he calls a halt.

'Easy there, lads, easy all!' He steps aside from the capstan, and looks over the rail. 'It'll take some storm to reach her now.'

The exhausted crew slump to the deck, blowing hard, while Simva tries to thank the Aleut with smiles and halting words.

Then Joshua rises to address them all, leaving pauses for Simva to translate. 'We have today given our ship a chance to sail again, and ourselves the hope of departure from this place, where we feared all was lost. There is much work to do, and do it we shall.' He turns to face the Aleut. 'But not before we eat. I say we roast that seal-meat right here on the beach, and we share it with you, our new friends, by way of thanks.'

* * *

Scoresby races round the beach in chase of rabbits only he can see. His aimless scurries put to flight the sharp-eyed gulls that sense food from the group of people gathered round their beach fire. Gideon watches the gulls' outlines grow fuzzy in the thin fog that drifts down the pass behind the beach. He's never known stillness like this.

Hunger and fatigue slow Scoresby from a mad gallop to a loping trot, and then a walk, as he approaches the people by the fire. He knows not to beg from his shipmates, and the Aleut know enough about dogs to pay him no mind: but they cannot take their eyes off Pirate, who perches on Zannah's shoulder, pecking at the peanuts she hands him.

The tallest of the Aleut says something in his guttural language: Zannah doesn't know if he's talking to her or to Pirate.

'Tukum says he likes your rainbow bird,' Simva translates. Then adds words of her own: 'It was he who pulled you from the surf.' She turns to Gideon. 'And he says he likes your wolf too.'

Zannah smiles and hands Tukum a nut. When he offers it to Pirate, the parrot takes it in his beak, exposing his purple tongue. Tukum grins and sticks out his own tongue.

Zannah stretches her arm towards her rescuer. Pirate accepts the invitation, and half-shuffles, half-hops along to her wrist, and then, with a quick beat of his wings, leaps on to Tukum's shoulder. His underwing feathers flash briefly but vividly blue, a teasing reminder of tropical skies. The Aleut gasp at the quick thrill of colour, and laugh at their chief, who sits, stiffly delighted to be so honoured by such a creature.

Pirate leans forward to his eager audience and opens his beak. Tukum thinks another nut is called for, but before he can offer it, this rainbow creature speaks: 'Quiet! Quiet the watch!'

The Aleut laugh louder still, even if they don't understand the order. The laughter rises further when Pirate takes Tukum's ear in his beak and nips it, before telling him again to hush; but it is quickly stilled.

Vincent, sitting opposite, rises suddenly to his feet, irritation written across his face. He glares through the smoke at the Aleut, and at Pirate. The Aleut look back at him, but sideways, for only Tukum will meet his eye. Gideon watches Tukum; Zannah watches Pirate, who's bobbing on his shoulder. Scoresby stares at the chunk of seal-meat that hangs from Vincent's hand.

Silence hangs heavy in the air. Jacques crosses himself. 'Un ange passe,' he whispers. But it is Pirate who speaks out. 'Beware the crow!' he squawks. 'Beware the crow!'

Vincent spins on his heel, hurls his meat to the shingle, and stomps off. There's an exhalation of pent-up breath all around, raising new clouds to merge with each other and the enshrouding fog.

The snap of bone and an appreciative growl from Scoresby tells everyone that he at least is happy with Vincent's leavings.

Gideon turns to Jacques. 'What was it you said just then?'

'Un ange passe. When zere is a sudden stop in our talking, like zat, we say it is because an angel passes by. Did you feel eem?'

Gideon looks up. A fog-softened eagle slips overhead, waiting, like the gulls, for their meal to end. He shakes his head.

'I felt something,' says Zannah, as she reclaims Pirate. She stares at Vincent's departing back. 'But it wasn't an angel.'

Within moments Vincent's swallowed by the thickening fog. Gideon shivers at the clammy chill the fog brings.

Simva chucks the last log on the dwindling fire. 'Your afternoon's work will have to warm you, Giddy.

There's precious little driftwood on these shores.'

She and her crew-mates start to pack away their outdoor kitchen, while Nathan hacks at the remains of the seal carcass. He passes half to Tukum, who begins to nod his thanks, but stops abruptly. He cocks his head, along with his kin. They've all heard something. Nathan looks around, but he sees only fog, thick enough now to shield the ship, and all he hears is the clatter of shingle and the mutter of his crew-mates. All noise and movement are stilled when the sound comes again, unmistakably now, and loud enough for even Rosa to hear. It is a deep and distant moan, a single note held low and long, like the foghorn of a far-off ship, but filled with a yearning no ship could know. Zannah and Gideon look to Simva for explanation. She turns to Tukum, but he, and all the Aleut, are gone, vanished suddenly and silently into the fog. Scoresby's gaze is fixed on the half-seal they've left behind in their haste.

Again and again comes the call, never nearer, but ever more mournful with each successive blast. The twins, like the rest of the crew, stare into the enveloping fog, as if the milky air might part, to reveal the source of this heart-gripping sound. But the fog only thickens further, and all they can do is listen in wonder, until at last the sound falters, and fades, and is gone.

Joshua's first to his feet. 'Whatever made such a din has not come to help us right our ship. That we must do ourselves. So let us look to it, one and all.'

CHAPTER 5
BEWARE THE CROW

GIDEON SIGHS, EXASPERATED IN EQUAL measure by his sister and the work they have been put to. He lowers his crude chisel to the planks beneath his prone body, squeezed in alongside Zannah's in the tight confines of the forwardmost crevices of the hold. 'All right,' he says. '*All right.*'

He raises his tattered knuckles to the dim light Nathan had rigged when he sent them forward. He wanted them to work within the hull to guide the skilled carpenters without, as they repair the sprung bow planking. He cannot tell if the blood smudge marks fresh lacerations or simply coats old cuts. He licks his knuckles clean, grimacing at the salty blood-and-sawdust taste. 'Maybe it wasn't a ship.' He turns to Zannah, her eyes bright in the dark hold beside him. 'What on earth was it then?'

'Nothing on *earth*, you walrus.' She gouges away with her own, sharper, chisel at the broken planks between them. 'And not "*maybe*" wasn't a ship. More "*could not have been*" a ship. There's no other ships for miles and miles. There's nothing here for them: there's no harbour. We only came by accident.'

'Rubbish, you sea-cow! I've seen the charts. Oonalashka's a day's sail away.'

'So?'

'Its other name is Dutch Harbour. Though what brings Dutchmen here is beyond me.'

Zannah pauses, before trying a different tack. 'But Giddy, we've heard foghorns before. None of them sounded like that. It wasn't a machine. It didn't come from anything made by people. Everyone heard it, and they all said the same.'

Giddy picks up his chisel and sets to work again, saying nothing. He lets her continue.

'The Aleut heard it first . . . and it was then that they vanished.' She attacks the planking again, and patters on, more to herself than her brother. 'It's as if they don't want anyone to know about it. But why not?'

There's a rapping and a muffled shout outside: Nathan. 'Enough there, twins! We can get a blade in now, so keep well away.'

On Gideon's side the tip of a saw enters where he has chiselled the broken plank away. Gideon shrinks back and presses up against his sister, as they both watch the saw and its progress.

The saw's rasp fills Gideon's left ear, as Nathan starts to cut: but his sister's whisper, on his right, is more insistent and somehow holds more threat.

'If I hear that noise again – fog or no fog – I'm off to find out what makes it,' she hisses. 'Will you come too?'

'They won't let you.'

'That's not stopped me – *us* – before.'

Gideon yelps as the saw bites his shoulder. Zannah pulls him tighter towards her, and away from the hull. 'I *have* to know,' she tells him.

Gideon puts a finger through the new hole in his jersey. 'What if we get lost?'

Zannah smiles. 'We'll take Scoresby. He'll sniff our way back, and bark away the bears.'

Zannah lets her mother go ahead, picking her way across the shingled shore, and looks back over her shoulder, the one Pirate's not perched on. For the first time in months her ship's out of sight, although a twist of woodsmoke marks the makeshift forge

Joshua's built on the beach nearby.

Zannah turns to look ahead. On her left, swirls of kelp-capped rocks push up through the waters' oily calm. Seabirds patrol the water-line, eager for whatever soft and salty delicacies their probing beaks can find in the barnacled crevices. Further out a solitary gull wheels low over the water, then folds its wings to attack its reflection in the mirrored surface, breaking through with a minimal splash to emerge, moments later, with a plump pink starfish clamped in its beak. After a failed effort to swallow its catch in a single greedy gulp, the bird paddles ashore to tear it into gull-gobblable pieces before other, hungrier, gulls can steal any.

Simva's watched all this and not broken her stride. When Zannah hurries to catch her up, the gull and the other seabirds take flight in alarm. Pirate follows, as if chasing them off, in a flaming blur of feathers, all scarlet and indigo against a pewter sky. He doesn't follow far before he peels off to inspect the writhing remnants of the starfish. It's not to his taste, but he needs some kind of trophy, so he's soon back on Zannah's shoulder, dangling a starfish leg by her ear.

Zannah pretends not to notice. 'I like this place,' she tells Simva. 'I don't know why. It's cold, and it's wild, and it's so far from the rest of the world.'

'Maybe that's why.'

'Why what?'

'Maybe that's why you like it. All this.' Simva extends one arm to the seascape, and the other to the hills piled up behind it. Only now does Zannah see the red-brown fox walking boldly through the yellow spring sedge. Pirate's seen him, too. 'Here boy!' he squawks, as if to a dog, and the starfish leg falls, still writhing, to the ground. Zannah kicks it away and shushes him with a sunflower seed.

'I like it too, Zannah. But it's no place for parrots. And this is the spring. How would you like to winter in a barbera like ours?'

'I'd like to find out what it's like. You already know.'

'True.' Simva hasn't wintered in barberas, but she was born in an igloo and she's lived on the ice in seal-skin tents. She knows everything there is to know about Northern winters.

'And you want to live it once more.'

True again, thinks Simva. She doesn't voice it: but Zannah's right.

'Why don't you say anything?' Zannah continues. She's not just talking about the moment, and the two of them. 'I would.'

'I know you would,' says Simva. 'But sometimes silence is the right course.'

'You told me once that every silence ends.'

'I did. And this one will. But at a time of my choosing.' Simva's tone makes clear that the time is not now.

Zannah changes the subject. 'What are their barberas like?'

'You'll see soon. Just beyond the headland: that's their village.'

They reach a cluster of barberas, scarcely noticeable until stood upon, and ranged around them are the markers of Aleut life: fish drying on racks; animal skins stretched over frames; a half-built kayak; the dog-gnawed bones of sea animals; and a scattering of tiny, intricate baskets made of woven grass. But there are no people.

Simva calls down each barbera's entrance ladder in turn, without reply. 'I don't understand,' she says, with a frown. 'I've been here three times now. They obviously live here, but they are never about.'

'They're at sea,' Zannah interrupts, pointing out a fleet of tiny kayaks half a mile offshore, drifting in the kelp beds and a slight swell. A silhouetted arm, bearing a harpoon, is raised and ready. But it is Simva who is struck, instantly transported down the decades and over the oceans to her own kayaking days, and especially the time she'd taught Joshua the precious skills.

'I'll come back' he'd told her: and he did: he came back for her. She made no such promise herself, for she knew she might never return. She's always missed her people keenly: but only now, on this Alaskan beach, does she fully know how much she still misses the life she led among them.

She watches the kayaks, feeling again in her shoulders and wrists the movement of the paddles, and, underneath her, the lift and chill of the fragile vessel as it rides the icy swell. She sees again the seals and the walrus she used to stalk and catch, and even, for a moment, the narwhal Joshua would not kill. She smells the blubber stoves, she tastes the meat, she breathes once more the air that crackles with cold, and she sighs. For Zannah's right: it still pumps in her blood, this northern life. All the tropical sunshine and palmy warmth she's shared with her husband, her children and crew, has not bleached any of its rich redness.

Zannah knows not to interrupt her mother's pensive silence on their way back to the *Unicorn*. She walks alongside, thoughts of her own chasing around her head: *The Aleut are avoiding us. They wouldn't all go to* sea, and abandon their village to hungry foxes and who knows what else. And where are their dogs? She looks up: the ship's in sight again. *The question is: why? What are they hiding?* She spies Vincent, at work in the stern. *Who are they hiding from?*

The sound of the rest of the crew labouring noisily on and around the ship, puts an end to Zannah's musings, but deepens Simva's silence. Hal's whistle and Kanaka's South Sea chant rise above the hammering, the sawing and the grunts of labour. The discordant racket loudens as they draw near, all except for the intense close-quarter talk between Vincent and Sven over the damaged steering gear. They work on, but in a watchful hush, as Simva and Zannah clamber up the gangplank.

'Any luck?' hails Joshua.

Simva simply shakes her head and Zannah replies for them both: 'Nobody home.'

The barbera's much homelier now. Rescued oil-lamps cast a warm light into all but the deepest recesses, where books and other precious materials are stored. Some of the crew have rigged hammocks, while others prefer the stability of low benches. Others still have volunteered to sleep on the ship, Vincent foremost amongst them, citing reasons of space. Some, especially Zannah, were glad of his offer, but uneasy that Sven had joined him. Kanaka had declined Vincent's invitation, saying he valued the warmth of the fire too highly to give it up.

Apart from brief midday breaks on the beach, everyone eats in the barbera, taking turns at the cooking and clearing up, as they do at sea. The chef changes more often than the menu, as Joshua's keen to conserve the stores left undamaged in the stranding.

Jacques stares at his plate. 'Zis is no diet for a man from Marseilles!' he exclaims, inspecting the indefinable lumps Nathan's just ladled out.

'When I get 'ome – a rich man at last – I will open a restaurant where I will cook nozzink bar seal meat an feesh, seal meat an feesh every day of ze week.' He looks around the assembled crew. 'I will call it Stranded Jacques. You can all come to ze opening night.'

Hal grins. 'And d'ye reckon there'll be custom after that?'

'I care not. I will not eat ze food maself, jus' make it for ozzers – while I gorge on Chateaubriand au poivre, and tarte aux pommes avec Chantilly – to remind me of zis 'ungry time at ze top of ze worl', and all ze reasons to be glad I'm on dry French land.'

Nathan brandishes a large knife and an accent more lethal. 'Ah am 'ead chef today, Monsieur le gourmet. You 'ave a complaint?'

'No no, mon brave. It is not ze cook; it is ze *ingredients*.'

Pirate's enjoying the banter, skipping from shoulder to shoulder and stealing titbits as he goes. Hal's laughing now, as are others around him. 'To really recreate the experience, your customers would have to build your bistro before they eat there.'

'From nothing but driftwood,' Nathan adds. 'With their bare hands, mind.'

'But zere's even less driftwood in Paris zan 'ere.'

'Unless you count the human kind,' Hal cuts in. Vincent stiffens. Whether it's because of Hal's quip or Pirate's sudden arrival on his shoulder, it isn't clear.

'Are you talking about me?' Vincent demands.

Hal blusters. 'I made a joke, is all. About Paris. The people there are even harder to reach than these Aleut.'

Vincent leans forward. 'I reckon you *were* talking about me.' Pirate doesn't notice the altered atmosphere; he only has eyes for the bright red end of Vincent's neck scarf, too tempting to ignore, so near at claw. He grasps it in his beak, and tugs. The knot gives, the scarf slips down, and Vincent's coiled tension is released.

He swipes at Pirate – 'That *damnable* bird!' – but Pirate evades his swinging fist, and Vincent's too busy scrabbling for his scarf in the dark alcove behind him to try again. Scoresby's on his feet in an instant, hurling himself forward in defence of his parrot companion. Only by grabbing the dog's collar as he flies past does Gideon save Vincent from a mauling.

It's all happened very fast, and the light is dim, but Gideon is sure nonetheless. Beneath Vincent's scarf is indeed a mark, and a large one at that, but too neat, too sharp-lined, and too blue-black to be a burn-scar, as he claimed. It could only be a tattoo, and a tattoo Vincent doesn't want noticed. Gideon looks at Zannah, but she's tending to Pirate, and hasn't seen. Nor it seems, has anyone else; when Vincent returns to the fireside and the circle of light, his scarf is now firmly in place, double-knotted and parrot-proof. Scoresby bares his teeth in a silent snarl, but submits to Gideon's will, and backs away to a distant corner, where Pirate soon joins him.

Vincent smiles like a snake, eyes flitting from face to face. 'Forgive me, ship-mates. Ever since that albatross I find the company of birds trying.' His apology is over, and his smile has gone, by the time he meets Hal's eye.

Joshua stands. 'Some grog is called for, I'd say.' He

nods to Gideon, who ducks into the alcove where the bottles are kept, and returns with a flask. A powerful aroma of molasses and rum spirit fills the chilly air as the flask is unstoppered and passed around, to splash the essence of Jamaica into proffered tumblers. Joshua waits till all are filled, then speaks. 'The spring tides are on us in a day or so, and we are nearly done –'

'In more ways than one!' Rosa interrupts, inspecting her ruined hands.

Joshua raises his tankard. 'She's ready to refloat. We'll sail her to Dutch Harbour for essentials –' Gideon sticks his tongue out at Zannah, who doesn't notice, for she's watching her mother – 'and thence to Japan and warmer climes. This is our furthest north. Let's drink a farewell to this mud hut and toast our return to the seas which are our home.'

Simva watches her husband throughout his speech, wincing at his words, and declines to join in the toast when he's done. Zannah, who'd begun by raising her glass of watered-down grog as high as her brother's beside her, finds her arm falling slowly to her side, and then clamped there by her father's description of their barbera refuge. A *mud hut*, he'd called it.

* * *

The weather's changing in Gideon's dream. He's lying on a Tahitian beach, counting coconuts in the trees above, when a chilling shadow first fuzzes over and then blocks out the sun. He rolls into the light and the warmth once more, but the shadow follows. He rolls again, till something warm and furry blocks him and breathes on his face. It is then he wakes up.

It takes a time for him to work out where he is, and for his sight to adjust. The feeble glow of the single night-lamp is reflected, intensely, in Scoresby's dark eyes. 'You've woken me up,' chides Gideon, in a whisper. 'But what's woken you?'

The answer comes quickly. For outside, above, he hears again the foghorn call like the one on the beach, which had so intrigued Zannah.

Gideon's gaze flashes across to her bunk: empty! He's about to fling back his furs and chase after her, when there's a creak from the ladder. There, halfway up, she stands, as still as she can, one hand beckoning, the other with a finger to her lips.

Gideon nods and grips Scoresby's collar. They watch as Zannah slowly steps up to the next notch. It creaks too, even more loudly, and there's a stirring in the nearby alcove, the one that Joshua and Simva share.

Gideon moans loudly, as if in a nightmare, and rolls

to his left, crashing on to the floor and Scoresby's tail with a loud 'ouch!' The dog yelps. In the commotion Zannah's swiftly up the steps, unnoticed, and soon swallowed by the woolly dark beyond.

'Gideon?' It's Simva's voice, thick with sleep.

'Just a nightmare. I'm fine,' he reassures her, as he quickly dons the furs that have served as his blanket. 'Call of nature, though. I'm just going outside.'

'Don't get lost.'

'I'll take Scoresby, if I may.'

'Good. I reckon he's safer outside.' This from Joshua. 'Then rest, son. The day's soon upon us and there's work to do.'

Simva sighs. 'There's always work to do.'

He's soon up the ladder, and in the middle of a call of nature (*This way I'm not lying*, he thinks) when he hears Zannah's hiss.

'Could you not wait till I'm finished?' he hisses back, when he joins her a little way above the barbera. She's dressed and ready, with a coil of rope over her shoulder and a driftwood staff in each hand. As she steps forward to pass him one, he sees the sheathed knife hung round her neck.

'What's that for?'

'You never know.'

'Never know what?'

'What we might find. Who we might meet.' And at that the foghorn sounds again, loud enough now to guess where from: over the pass. 'Let's go.' Zannah hands him a staff and sets off.

Overnight frost has glazed the moonlit snow with a thin crust of ice, where the previous day's thawing sun reached the south-facing slopes of the pass. Boy, girl and dog feet crunch through to varying depths of powdery snow beneath. After first Scoresby and then Zannah have disappeared completely in the deep drifts that fill the valleys, they decide to climb near the crest of a wind-scoured ridge, on the moonlit side.

Each time the foghorn sounds they stop, to check for direction, and to rest. On one such break, Gideon looks up. Stars glitter like ice-points high overhead, and the spring-tide full moon gilds the ridges, spilling purple-black shadow into the valleys on either side.

'Why a foghorn but no fog?' asks Zannah.

Gideon lowers his gaze and listens. In between the haunting calls, once his breathing eases, he can hear the trickle of a stream, deep in the valley, and hidden by snow. He tracks the sound upwards, to the head of the pass, and points.

'There's no fog *here*. But look.'

Zannah follows his indicating arm. At the very summit of the pass, cupped between the mountains on either side, stands a woollen wall, like a fuzzy dam a hundred feet high. The fog-bank blots out the stars behind and sucks up the moonlight like a sponge: but it stands, piled up against its limit, as if forbidden to descend the valley in anything other than token wisps.

'Must be a sea-fog coming up from the Northern shore, the other side of the island,' says Gideon.

'Remember how, when the noise came before, the fog spilled down, all of a sudden?' his sister asks.

Gideon nods. 'We'd better rope up,' he says.

Zannah's already uncoiled the rope and made one end fast round her waist. She fashions a loop which she attaches to Scoresby's collar, and hands the other end to Gideon.

They climb on, in single file, throwing huge shadows on to the next crest, which dance, when they slip on the ice, or vanish, when they drop into drifts. They soon feel the clammy weight of the fog about them. The shadows vanish. The stars have gone and the moon is dim.

They pause, waiting for the call. Each time it comes

they set off towards it, planting heavy feet to allow them to retrace their steps. Gideon concentrates on Scoresby's rippling shoulders, his fur beaded with fog moisture like finely crafted chain mail. When the fogcalls come Gideon watches the movement in Scoresby's neck and the twitch of his pricked-up ears, to confirm his own sense of their origin.

They are soon heading down, and steeply too. The foghorn calls are louder now, despite the muffled air, and the yearning within them is ever more urgent. Boy and girl and dog are drawn on and down. Something powerful in the noise that booms about the slope seems to grip and pull them to it: something so strong it is all they can do not to break into a blind and tumbling rush, which could take them over any cliff or precipice lying ahead.

The lower they go, the clearer it becomes that there is not one call; but a chorus of them, all blasting together, in an unearthly choir. And then, just as it seems they must be upon the source, or sources, of these calls, Gideon and Zannah drop through the fog floor to clear air and a spectacle to clutch their hearts. They stand atop a low cliff, still snow-dusted, looking down on a bay much like their own, although this one faces North. No swell comes in from the Bering Sea beyond, there being not a wisp of wind. The fog thins and rises, though odd wreaths linger, hanging motionless in the still still air. But the water boils. The surface is broken by surges and splashes and spray, churned up from below by a teeming mass of creatures. Barnacled backs, waving fins, and thrashing tail flukes show above the tumult in numbers beyond counting.

Then comes the loudest and the last call, a tremendous ringing blast which echoes round the rocks. The churning eases. The waters settle. The backs and fins and flukes move out to sea and slip beneath the surface. The calls come no more; they are gone with the fog.

Gideon and Zannah look on, amazed. Within minutes the water is slate-smooth once more, reflecting the sparkle of fog-freed stars and the grey-pink blush of dawn to the east.

The twins are lost for speech till Zannah, seeing Gideon pinch himself, gasps, 'Yes, Giddy. They were really here.'

'Whatever they were . . .'

'They're what the Aleut don't want us to see. And now we have.'

'But who'll believe us? It's already hard to believe it myself.'

'We won't tell.'

'We'll have to say something.'

They trudge back up the hill, almost outpacing the rising base of the fog-bank. Gideon's impressed how straight their downhill tracks have been. He ruffles Scoresby's ears: 'Well done, boy!'

But Scoresby's unhappy. He looks about, left and right, then dashes ahead, tugging the twins he's still roped to, until he's sniffing at their outward tracks. 'What is it?' asks Gideon: but the answer's clearly written in the snow. For as well as the trail of two twins, and the plantings of their staffs, and the pad-marks of their dog, there are other, deeper footprints, much bigger than their own. They've been followed.

Gideon grips his staff and Zannah her knife. They stare about, unable to decide whether to rush uphill for the cover of the fog-bank, or to stay well below it to see who their pursuer might be. The fog-bank chooses for them, by continuing to rise until it clears the summit of the pass.

They climb on, warily, checking for more tracks, or their maker, till they reach the ridge. They can see, by the early light, the Southern bay with their stranded ship laid out below.

'There!' Zannah tugs Gideon's sleeve and falls to

the snow. Not far off, dropping fast down a valley to the east, and shrinking into the shadow, is a wiry figure whose loping wolf-like walk she would know anywhere. 'Vincent!'

They wait until he's reached the shore and lost to sight, then follow him down in the rising light, till they are nearly upon their barbera. Smoke, breakfast smells, and the sounds of rousing people ascend from the roof window and ladder-gap. Vincent suddenly appears from the shore side, as they approach from the hill, and arrives at the entrance before them.

'Excellent work, youngsters,' he hails them loudly, projecting his voice into the barbera below. 'A grand start we've made.' His friendly tone disarms Scoresby enough to let him reach the ladder, where he drops two steps and turns, so his sharp-eyed face is level with the astonished twins. He lets his jacket fall open just enough to show the butt of a pistol tucked into his belt, leans forward, and hisses at Gideon.

'You breathe a word of what you have seen, sonny, and I will make you pay. Dearly.' His eyes slide sideways to Zannah, and a cruel half-smile plays across his mouth. He turns to Gideon again. 'No I won't. I'll make *her* pay.'

There's suddenly a knife in his hand, and his hand's at Gideon's throat. He looks at Zannah. 'The same goes for you, girlie. One word and you've a brother no more.'

A low growl from Scoresby has the knife back in his pocket in a flash, and he slides down the ladder.

'Good workers, your twins,' he booms to Simva, heartier than they've ever heard him. 'I've been a stranger to sleep since that open boat, and what do I hear, long before dawn, but young Giddy and Zannah humping stores down the beach, ready for loading. We've all worked up an appetite for breakfast.'

Gideon and Zannah listen from above, suddenly aware of their shivers.

His voice booms upwards. 'Haven't we, twins?'

They don't – they can't – speak at first, but he calls up again, in a voice that is chilling in its cheeriness.

'That's right. Hungrier than ever before,' says Gideon, trying to put conviction in his wooden voice.

Zannah backs him up. 'Is there porridge?'

Gideon looks at her, before leading the way down. 'There will be a way,' he insists, quietly. 'We'll find one.' She nods.

While they wait for the tide to rise underneath their ship, the *Unicorn*'s crew run lines out from the capstans and over the stern, to outlying rocks in the bay, then set greased skids behind her.

'She's all set to go,' says Nathan to Zannah on the beach. 'We'll load the lighter stuff now – these boxes here. Heavy goods and ballast once she's afloat.'

Together they lift one of the boxes, while Zannah casts glances about. All morning, she and Gideon have looked for a moment to approach Joshua or Simva in safety, and out of Vincent's view. But whenever one of them gets close, Vincent's right next to the other, looking intently across. Zannah wonders if he's watching her near Nathan now. Her heart jumps when she sees Vincent, alone on the bow of the ship. Here's a chance.

She drops the box. 'Nathan . . .'

There's a cough to her left, where Gideon stoops over a load of his own. Right next to him, and watching them both, is Sven. One of his huge hands reaches inside his jacket, and he shakes his head very slowly.

'What is it, lassie?' Nathan asks.

Something glints in Sven's hand. Zannah pauses, then arches her back with a wince. 'Sorry . . . It's my back. All this lugging.'

The loading goes on all day, and throughout it, unnoticed by anyone else, Gideon, Zannah, Vincent and now Sven, pursue their elaborate dance of movement, looks and gesture; until the tide's right in, and it's all hands to the capstan to winch her off the beach. Vincent makes sure he shares a capstan bar with Gideon, and Sven with Zannah. 'Not a word, boy, unless it's to sing us a shanty,' says Vincent, with a grin, and loud enough for all to hear. Gideon looks at him. He suddenly can't remember any songs.

Kanaka starts one up, a familiar mixture of English, his own Polynesian, and grunts which sound the same in any tongue.

It's hard at first, but with the ripples of the rising tide, and muscles united by song, the ship starts to slip over the skids and down the beach, in a move mirroring that which brought her up there a fortnight before. Once her stern starts to float the work gets lighter, and the crew spin round the capstan ever faster, till the movement underfoot tells them she's refloated, and a ship again at last. She bobs in the dying light of the day.

Zannah and Gideon don't join in the cheers that ring around them. When Nathan's checked below for leaks, and the ship's secured by anchors, bow and stern, well out in the bay, Joshua calls a halt. 'Enough for one day!' he says. 'We'll finish loading tomorrow, and then at last we can leave.'

Scoresby leads the way back from the beach. He's

watched while others worked, he's hungry, and he's keen for some parrot company, so he makes sure he's first. He half climbs, half falls down the ladder, with Zannah soon after, and Sven not far behind.

Rosa greets the dog. 'Home and hungry, eh? But where's Pirate?'

Zannah catches her breath and freezes as she steps off the ladder. 'I thought he was with you.'

'No, love. And I've been here for hours.'

Zannah shoulders Sven aside and scrambles back up. Once above, she runs, without knowing where, heedless of the shouts behind her, and only one thought in her head: *Vincent*.

She's soon on to the snow, heading east, parallel to the shore, looking wildly about. There's a panting and pattering behind her, which has her alarmed, till Scoresby catches up and runs alongside.

Down on the shore, Vincent watches Gideon closely. But Gideon hears his sister's shouted name, and he's quicker by just enough to evade Vincent's grasp. He dashes over weed-slippy rocks to the turf above the beach, where he breaks into a run to try and head off his sister. Vincent gives chase for a while, till he thinks better of it, and heads up to the barbera.

Gideon races at an angle up on to the snow, calling

to Scoresby and Zannah to stop. Neither heeds him. He hurls himself at Zannah's whirling feet as she passes, and they tumble headlong into a drift. Panting hard, Gideon clings to his sister's kicking legs, refusing to let her go. When breath returns he yells at her: 'What is it? *Tell* me.'

The kicking stops, and she replies in short bursts of speech, punctuated by gasps. 'Pirate ... Gone ... *Vincent* ... Knew it ... All along.' Some of the gasps sound like sobs now.

Gideon lets her go.

'And now I know it too. We must get back and tell them.'

Zannah beats the snow off her furs with angry blows. 'Not till we find Pirate. Vincent'll spin them a story unless we can prove it.'

Scoresby's already padding about, sniffing at the ground. After weeks on the site, and no fresh snowfall, there's a confusing mixture of tracks, leading off in every direction.

'Scent doesn't linger on snow,' says Zannah, suddenly calm.

'Not unless it's new. If anyone can find him, Scoresby will.'

So they scour the shore and the hillside, in the

gathering gloom, trying to nudge what pattern they can into Scoresby's searching. It's fully dark, and growing crisply cold, when Scoresby's meanderings suddenly show more purpose and direction, and his bark tells them he's on to something. It's all they can do to keep up as Scoresby races up the slope, nose to the ground, towards an outcrop of rocks, where he disappears from view. There's a moment's silence, and then a heart-wrenching howl that echoes round the hills and out to sea.

Gideon and Zannah turn past the biggest boulder. Scoresby sits, his snow spattered snout pointing at the fat full moon. He lets out another eerie howl in a cloud of silver breath, then looks down at the pitiful bundle by his forepaws. Pirate's body lies broken on the moonlit snow, and scattered around him, like fallen petals in a rose garden, is a rainbow of brilliant feathers.

Zannah falls to her knees, and slips off her gloves. With one bare hand she clutches Scoresby's thick shoulder fur, and with the other she strokes Pirate's outstretched intact wing.

Gideon paces around, his resolve for revenge strengthening with each feather he picks from the snow and stuffs into his pocket. He reaches down to a red splash, only to find his fingers sink into slushy parrot blood. He covers it over before Zannah sees, then jabs his fingers into the snow, over and over, to clean them off.

'We can't even bury him, the ground's so hard,' Zannah says with bitterness.

'No. But we can mark the place.'

They dig a hole in the snow, down to the iron-hard soil, lay Pirate in it, and solemnly cover him over. Gideon fills the hole with rocks, which he piles up in a flat-topped pyramid cairn. He lays three of Pirate's largest feathers – red, green and blue – on top, then lowers a last rock to hold them in place. 'No storm will blow this loose,' he says, turning to Zannah.

She fingers her knife, still slung round her neck, and looks back with tear-filled eyes. 'I'm going to kill him,' she says, quietly, and only once; but Gideon knows she means it. He wonders if he means it too.

There's little urgency in their silent trudge back to the barbera until Gideon feels in his hair the first tug of wind there's been for days. 'Northerly,' he murmurs. 'A good wind to leave by.' He looks across towards the *Unicorn*: and stops in mid-stride, amazed to see the sails on her remaining mast spill down, one after another, and the ship gather speed and sail out towards the head of the bay.

Gideon yells, a huge incoherent roar of betrayal and dismay, and hurtles off downhill. He is closely followed by Zannah, who's roused rapidly from her distress, and joins him in his banshee screech. Scoresby barks his own mixed cry of alarm and revenge.

The puzzled crew clamber up from the barbera, and when they see their ship make off without them, give vent to shouts of their own and run towards the rocks that guard the bay's entrance. Joshua drops back down the ladder, to re-emerge with a rifle, which he loads as he makes for the headland.

Gideon pants to his father, 'It's Vincent. Sven too.'

'Killed Pirate,' gasps Zannah, on his other side.

Gideon's at full tilt, while Joshua's jogging. Only when he sees his father drop to one knee and place his rifle on the boulder before him, does he understand that he's been saving his breath, the better to shoot straight. The ship's picking up speed, and although the moon is low and bright, there will only be time for one or two shots as she passes by. Joshua has to make them tell.

Shouts and curses fill the air as the crew rages furiously at the very water's edge, where the ship slips by. They are suddenly stilled by a shot. The wood of the helmwheel between the helmsman's hands splinters, and the helmsman turns with a terrible snarl. When they see it is Sven, the shouts rise again, but there's a flash from the darkness near the mast, as another shot rings out,

146

this time from the ship, forcing them all to dive for what cover they can find. Gideon sprawls on the shingle beside his father, who is taking careful aim.

Now that he has the range he cannot miss, even if Vincent's firing back. Gideon watches the tension rise in his father's trigger finger, and covers his ears. There's a long long pause, marked by the movement of the gun as Joshua tracks his target. Then a despairing sigh. 'I cannot shoot him,' says Joshua. 'I cannot.'

From the ship there's another shot, spraying rock chips where it hits the sheltering boulder, and a roar of mocking laughter, equally sharp. 'You are weak, Captain Murphy, and your ship is now mine.'

A fish harpoon slams into the mast above Vincent's head. He dashes forward to see Aleut kayaks arrayed before him, in a sweeping arc. Some have harpoons raised, and set in throwing boards. Others are closing in with grapnel hooks and lines, ready to board the vessel.

The *Unicorn* bears down on them, and they on it. Joshua moves to a different boulder and settles his aim on Vincent at the bow sprit. But there's someone else there, holding a lantern high overhead to show him and all the kayakers his face. His Aleut face; bruised and bleeding; and with Vincent's pistol cocked and pressed up against his temple.

Vincent shouts something in Aleut at the kayaks ahead. Gideon needs no translation to know his meaning: that he has hostages.

'Four of them,' says Simva. 'He'll kill them all and sail the ship himself if he has to.'

Tukum, whose harpoon's now part of the ship, gestures to his fleet, on either side. The harpoon hands are lowered, and the grapnel hooks unswung. The line of kayaks parts reluctantly, just enough to allow the ship through, and forms again in her wake. Vincent drags his victim back to the stern rail as the ship moves on, daring anyone to defy him. No one does.

And then, when he's sure no harpoon can reach him, he hurls his hostage to the deck, and, almost casually, drops his aim and fires at Tukum in the lead kayak.

There's a cry of pain and a splash as the kayak capsizes. The other Aleut paddle swiftly to his rescue, but despite their struggles, cannot right the big man's boat. Joshua hands his rifle to Nathan and strips off his outer furs and seaboots. He runs to the cold black water and plunges in, followed closely by Hal.

Gideon and Zannah watch the frantic melee of circling kayaks, spinning paddles, splashing arms and bobbing heads, making their way to shore. The twins move forward, wading in up to waist deep, until hauled back by Simva.

The kayak is still upturned, but three men cling to it and each other, and other kayaks support it at bow and stern. Tukum is sprawled over the hull, with Hal to port, supporting his legs, and Joshua to starboard, keeping his head out of the water. Ominous rivulets of blood, black in the moonlight, run from under Tukum's motionless body down the kayak's sides and into the sea.

Helping hands haul men and boats ashore, and in moments Hal and Joshua lie shivering under piles of fur from Aleut and castaway crew alike. Between them, silent and still, is Tukum, with a fellow kayaker pumping at his stomach and Nathan doing what he can to staunch the bleeding from his shoulder wound.

Tukum gives a cough, spluttering foamy seawater from his mouth; and then another, and then sits up. He watches Nathan cut away his sleeve, and when he sees the wound is not so bad as all the blood makes it look, he says something in Aleut. Gideon catches a word he's heard before: 'Promyshleniki', as Tukum looks around. His eyes settle on Zannah and then close as he starts to feel the pain from his wound and the loss of his kin. All other eyes now turn to the horizon, where the stolen ship and her hostage crew sail slowly off into the darkness.

CHAPTER 6
GREMYKOFF, MENDER OF CLOCKS

THERE'S SO MUCH SPLASHING FROM Zannah's paddles that she does not notice the kayak until its beak-like bow appears close alongside her cockpit. She turns, surprised to see Tukum and Attu catch up so soon. She's about to launch into some of the new Aleut words she's learnt, when she's brought up short by Joshua's gesture from the other cockpit behind her. He's stopped paddling, and holds a finger firmly to his lips.

In the third kayak, a little further ahead, Gideon and Simva chat and paddle on until shushed by Tukum's eider duck call. All three boats then drift silently, in the the westerly breeze, towards the kelp beds ahead, half a mile off the next headland.

It's early yet, so the summer sun lies low in the Eastern sky, and a golden glare sparkles off the water. Zannah shields her eyes and looks around. She can no longer see anything of her new home, Barbera Bay, five miles behind, or any sign at all that the island is peopled. All but the topmost snow is gone, and eagles soar over hillsides glowing with the luminous green of young summer grass. To starboard stretches the ocean, gentle-mooded today. Cormorants skim low over the steady swell, which breaks against the shore with the sound of giants breathing.

Zannah envies the caps worn by Attu and Tukum, not so much for their decoration of eagle feathers and walrus ivory, but their foot-long curved peaks. Normally serving as shields against rain, salt spray, wind, today they ward off a rare excess of sunshine. When Tukum turns, she sees again how the cap gives him enough of the profile of a large waterbird to deceive any unwary seal or walrus prey.

Tukum points with his paddle towards the kelp beds, and then Zannah sees what he'd spotted long before. Among the waving fronds, low in the water, and disappearing in the troughs of the swell, are six or seven dark shapes, each several feet long. Most lie like driftwood, rising and falling with the waves, but otherwise motionless. Two are more active, rolling and twisting themselves over and over amid coils of kelp. One drifts apart from the others. When she hears the steady tap-tap-tap it makes Zannah is finally sure what they are: otters. She and Gideon have seen them from the shore, but never this close; and never from the water. She smiles across at her brother, who's seen them too and is smiling back.

The animals seem unconcerned by their approach: the driftwood sleepers sleep on, securely bound in their kelp-curl beds. Zannah sees now that the twisters are just waking up, and their wriggling is an effort to uncoil themselves and greet the day. Finally free, one of them gives a single harsh cry, and leaps upon the other, rolling it over and over in wake-up play. The tap-tap sound comes from the early riser, which is already bashing open breakfast shellfish on a flat stone balanced on its belly. It gobbles up the yellow-orange contents, gazing without apparent concern at the approaching kayaks. And then, when they cross a threshold distance, it rolls over abruptly, dropping its anvil into the water, and barks a warning call to its tribe. The other otters stop their roll-play and turn to watch. A sleeping otter opens one eye, then returns to its dozes, trusting its sentries to warn of any real danger.

The wind pushes the kayaks slowly past, until a renewed tap-tap-tapping, now in triple time, indicates that otter breakfast is resumed. Tukum takes up his paddling again, and leads the little fleet out to sea. From behind, Gideon notices the slight catch in Tukum's otherwise smooth paddling; a contrast to Attu's effortless swing, and the only legacy, apart from his still-raw scars, of Vincent's bullet, back in the spring.

Gideon and Zannah have begged since then to accompany Joshua on his visits to Dutch Harbour, but always in vain: so when, last night, Joshua announced a trip to mark midsummer's day, it came as a surprise. He has been twice before: once with Nathan, once with Simva, and both times guided by Attu, the best Aleut kayaker. The twins have kayaked enough now, in singles and doubles, to know how to handle the boats inshore: but Dutch Harbour means an open sea passage to the next island, and they've seen from shore how fiercely the storms can roar, out in the strait.

This morning the weather is fine, the barometer steady, and the day the longest of the year. The twins' delight was only diminished by their concern for Scoresby. Quiet and subdued ever since Pirate's murder, he's always anxious when apart from one twin or the other, and they've never both been away together. Hal promised to take him fishing, and so they set off, each in the bow seat of a double kayak, provisioned for a two-day trip ('to town' as Joshua put it), in search of any word of their ship, or another they could make their own.

After another hour's paddling Tukum and Attu pause again, this time to survey the channel ahead before they finally leave the shelter of land. The swell, a dying remnant of an earlier storm, runs with the westerly wind, speeding them along their course. There's not a single whitecap, and the water glints invitingly in a golden road to the shores of Oonalashka.

Tukum looks to Simva, who smiles, and to Joshua, who nods, then points his paddle towards a distant line of forbidding cliffs, topped by a serene but non-smoking volcano.

'Makushin,' breathes Gideon, looking up at the conical slopes.

'Giddy the Navigator!' says Simva, well aware of the dark hours he and Joshua spent huddled over the few charts Vincent didn't steal.

'Surely we can't land there?'

'No. But if we steer towards it the tide will push us northwards, and all the way round to the bay.'

Gideon nods, but with a frown: he should know that.

The charts are old, and their accuracy in doubt; but they indicate clearly which way the tides run. Has he forgotten so soon?

'Here.' Simva hands him the flask of meltwater she filled at dawn, in an effort to quench his self-reproach. Gideon drinks eagerly. It's still ice-cold. He takes another mouthful and passes it back, mindful of the same ritual in the other kayaks on either side.

No signal is given, but they all resume paddling together, and the flotilla sets out to sea. Tukum and Attu cruise just ahead, with a twin on each quarter, puffing and splashing away.

'Listen to you!' Simva chides Gideon. 'It's not a race. You must paddle smooth and steady and let the boat do the work.'

'Do as she says, son.' Joshua's all smiles. 'For she teaches well. Did she not teach me when we were as young as you are now?'

Simva laughs to remember his first floundering efforts, in the icy waters of Greenland long ago, till a salt splash from Gideon's paddle shocks her back to the present, leaving an empty echo where her memory settles.

Once Zannah learns to relax into a rhythm, she's free to exult in the work of her shoulders, and the hum of her little boat as it speeds through water. Made as it is of once living sea-creatures, the flex in the seal-sinew lashings and the drum-like tension in the hide of the hull give the kayak renewed and vigorous life, as if it could surge along alone and unpaddled. She's seen the blood-red line painted inside the kayak, where the deck meets the sides, and heard from Tukum and Attu how this, the spirit line, marks the soul of the boat. Only now does she understand how a boat can have a soul: and she glories in it.

Zannah thrills to feel the stern lift, as each wave rolls underneath, and she surfs down the east-facing water slopes, paddling briskly to keep her craft straight. *So this is how water-beasts feel,* she thinks, as the next wave sweeps by, and her bow points skywards. She lifts her head, like a spy-hopping seal, and lets out a seal-call, a lowing hymn to the world of water around her and the shores of her new island home.

A sharp tap on her shoulder brings her back. Joshua doesn't say anything: he doesn't need to. The sinister black triangles are plain for all to see, even if they're a mile away. As tall as a man, they cut through the water, raising a white wave ahead to match the flashes they proudly bear near their trailing edges. A pod of killer whales, speeding North, into the Bering Sea.

Gideon holds up a non-paddling hand, fingers splayed to show he counts five.

'More, I think,' whispers Simva and quietly paddles on, watching them intently.

Zannah, chastened, stays silent. Moments before she had wanted nothing so much as to be a seal. Now, near these hunters, she's not so sure . . .

'Don't worry,' Joshua tells her. 'The seals they eat never see them coming. They're on passage, like us, bound for a different sea.'

Zannah watches them, all the same, counting them over and over as they glide North, till she can no longer pick them out in the vastness of the sea.

Mighty Makushin lies far behind, obscured by nearer peaks; and the sun is on its long glide down from its own furthest north. Gideon's getting tired. Steady paddling works up an unfamiliar sweat, but whenever he stops to remove a layer of clothing, he chills down quickly, even on this midsummer afternoon.

His eyes are fixed ahead: there's something he *must* see first, before anyone else. And there it is at last – a gaunt black pillar of rock a hundred feet high, standing apart from the cliffs behind it, utterly ungreened, and splashed at its throat by seabird guano. 'Priest Rock!' he calls in triumph: he's found the landmark for their turn into Dutch Harbour.

'Well done Giddy,' Joshua calls across. 'Not far now.'

They turn to starboard and hug the shoreline of the headland, as it falls away to the south: and suddenly they see the bay open up before them, a perfect natural harbour, sheltered on all sides.

Gideon gasps: after months of empty ocean and sparse shores, ahead there swing at anchor more ships than he can count, and people by the score. Boats ply to and from the shore beyond, and the air rings with hammering and sawing and the shouts of shipwrights in a babel of languages.

The kayaks weave along canyons formed by ships towering high on either side. Gideon and his sister scan them all, for names, for flags of nationality, for home port badges. Here's an exploration ship, low in the water and heavy-set for butting ice floes on its way to the Pole. There's the *Prince Victor*, a scruffy Russian fur trader. Moored alongside is *Helcia*, a battered packet boat from San Francisco, and out of place so far north. More out of place still are a British man-o-war, all guns and bright paint, and a Japanese whaler with its slanting sails.

Bearded men look down from every deck on the tiny kayaks far below. There's such a cold and greedy hardness in most of their eyes that the twins soon stop looking back. Simva, Tukum and Attu stare fixedly ahead, and paddle stony-faced. Only Joshua stares about him: and only he speaks. 'Any word of the *Unicorn*?' he calls. 'I seek my ship: the *Unicorn*.'

A Russian points at Joshua's kayak, and laughs to his deck-mates, then jeers down in heavily accented English. 'But you are in your ship, *Ingelski*, and a sorry sight it is.'

Cruel laughter rains down, raising a heat in Zannah's cheeks, and a flash in Gideon's eye. They're beginning to understand why the Aleut are so wary of these men they call the *promyshleniki*. The twins look to each other, to confirm that their anger is shared; and it is — but for different reasons. Zannah resents invasion: *how dare you barbarian outsiders taunt us Aleut, true stewards of these islands?* But Gideon seeks vindication: *we are true seafarers, and will have a ship again, nobler than any you rabble will ever crew.*

Joshua shouts something back in Russian, and the laughter stops. The kayaks paddle on, followed by cold stares, till they reach the shore.

A shingle beach runs across the head of the bay, and

behind it straggle lines of drab huts, scruffily built of clapboard and logs. Loose dogs wander amid a litter of seal-bones and driftwood. On a slight rise to the right stands a building unique in its height and colour. Two storeys high, with a tower rising above the main entrance another two storeys still, its walls gleam white under rich red roofs. The tower is topped by a bulbous dome, painted blue-grey, and itself surmounted by a white and gold cross unlike any the twins have seen before. It has three bars, the lowest slanting steeply: and perched atop the cross, as if surveying its kingdom, is a great eagle, looking haughtily down at these new arrivals.

Joshua waits while Attu and Tukum disembark, to be greeted and dragged aside by their Aleut kin. He guides his boat in to the landing place, where he beaches the bow on a patch of shelving sand. Zannah balances the boat with her paddles while her father gets out, and he then splashes forward to do the same for her. She stretches stiffened legs across lapping wavelets, and stands for the first time in hours. She and Joshua drag their boat clear for Simva to land after them, then set about unloading it of provisions and securing it against any sudden winds.

It's a short walk to the church of the eagle, but long

enough for them to stumble across two bodies in the grass. One clutches an empty bottle, in a hand bearing old white scars and new red wounds. The other's face is bruised and swollen. Both snore loudly, and there rises above them a mingled stench of stale sweat, old tobacco, and cheap vodka, which is strong enough to keep even the hungriest dog well away. Simva looks down with disdain as she steps between them, tugging Zannah past. 'Drunks,' says Joshua. 'No one drinks like the Russians.'

They lay their bags of possessions on the wooden verandah before the church, and step in through the wide open door. The twins look around in awe, as the dim light reveals the riches within. The white painted walls are hung everywhere with dark painted pictures in heavy gold frames. Candleholders bigger than cartwheels hang on gold chains from the roof. A richly carved lectern holds a heavy leather bible, guarded by a gilded eagle with wings spread wide. The light dims further, as a huge figure puts out the candles on the altar, one by one. A smell of candle wax and incense fills the air, and wick smoke drifts across beams of light slanting through the narrow windows set high in the wall.

Hearing their entrance, the figure turns, and seems to grow taller still. He wears heavily decorated robes, a magnificent flowing beard, and a strange hat that adds a foot to his already imposing height.

He smiles broadly, and speaks, first in Russian, then Aleut, and finally, when he recognises Joshua, in English.

'Welcome, welcome, Captain Murphy.' His voice is deep and booming, and he spreads his arms wide. 'All are welcome.'

'Father Gremykoff, this is Simva, my wife.'

Simva bows her head, and speaks in Aleut, broadening the enormous man's enormous smile still further. She turns to introduce the twins, using their full names.

'Taluqlika Susannah.' Zannah smiles nervously. 'And Gideon Kalatunah.' The priest lays a massive hand on, and almost around, each of their heads. Gideon feels the power throb within it, like the paw of some great bear.

'Fine children. I've heard much about you.'

Zannah indicates the rich decor all around. 'Ulax Tukuu,' she says brightly. 'A house fit for a chief,' she translates, for Gideon, with an air of superiority he finds irritating.

The priest's impressed. 'How quickly you learn! It is indeed a fine house, but it belongs not to me or any chief. It is God's house: Ulax Qugam, you might say.'

Zannah tries it out 'Ulax Qugam!'

'Precisely so. And that means it is open to everybody.

My own house is close by.' He turns to Joshua. 'And you must all lodge there this night.'

He stills Joshua's protests with a gesture. 'No, no. I wish to enjoy the company of you and your family. It will be a pleasure for me.'

He disappears into a small robing room, and re-emerges moments later looking much like one of the Russian seamen who had abused them. He leads them out of the church, clutching a large empty wooden bucket. When they pass again the drunks, he hands the bucket to Gideon and bids him fill it with seawater, and then stand well back as he douses each drunken head with a gallon of chilly brine.

The drunkards rouse, spluttering and roaring like wounded walruses, and stagger to their feet, instantly resuming the fight that had been curtailed by the onset of their stupor. The one with the bottle takes a swig at it, and then, finding it empty, wields it as a club, swinging feebly at his foe. The priest grabs his arm, tears the bottle from his wrist, and tosses it into the sea, then takes each man by the collar and runs them down the beach, letting go at the water's edge, and hurling them forward full length into the shallows. He calls to them in Russian, and wheels away, unafraid to turn his back on two violent drunkards he has so provoked.

'What did you say to them?' asks Zannah, as he strides back up the beach.

'That they must come to the church when they are sober and seek forgiveness.'

'What if they do not forgive you?' asks Gideon, as he gazes on the splashing men, still roaring in the water.

'I am a man of peace,' says Gremykoff. 'Look.'

And where before these two had threatened murder, now they have arms linked like Cossack dancers. They stumble back up the beach and out of the water. One has found the discarded bottle, half full again, but only of seawater. He takes a swig, swallows with a hidden grimace, and hands it to his partner, who downs a huge draught before spraying it out like a spouting whale. There's a pause that threatens more violence, before both men fall into fits of ribald laughter, and collapse in each other's arms on the shingle.

The priest's house is as small and simple as his church is large and ornate. The logs and pine boards are mostly unpainted, and now glow golden in the summer evening light that streams through rarely opened windows. A housekeeper hovers, looking much like an elderly Aleut woman, but introduced by Gremykoff as

Anya, a Siberian. The awe in her eyes shows that she sees him as a kind of God, rather than a mere man in the service of the church. 'Anya goes wherever the church sends me,' says Gremykoff in a kindly tone. 'It is decades now since she's seen the banks of the Lena, or the birch trees of home.'

Anya pours tea from the gleaming brass samovar, then busies herself in the kitchen. Gideon's aware of something that intrudes upon the quiet stillness of the house: a steady whirr like the drone of sleepy bees.

Gremykoff watches Gideon look around and settle on the door in the corner as the source of the sound. 'My workshop,' he says, 'where I make and mend. And tonight – your berths.' Gideon turns to Zannah. They exchange curious glances.

Gremykoff smiles to himself, then has them all sit round his bare wooden table, darkened and scarred with age. In the silence that begins and ends his grace, solemnly spoken in Russian, the buzz behind the door seems to louden. Gideon wonders what he is to share his cabin with.

Anya serves brimful bowls of stew, each centred on a heavy flour dumpling, while Gremykoff slices a loaf of dense black bread and passes it around. Gideon beams at him: he's not eaten at table since the *Unicorn* was driven ashore. He'd forgotten how much he missed it. 'Thank you,' he says, and then, remembering the Russian: 'Spasibo,' as he takes the offered bread. He immediately regrets the word, when he sees the look on Zannah's face.

Gremykoff's seen it too. 'Our Russian bread is not to your liking?' Zannah lowers the slice to her plate. Her mouth has gone suddenly dry; but her eyes are moist.

Gideon rescues her. 'We had a parrot, Father. He spoke some Russian. *Spasibo* was his favourite word.'

'Was?'

'He's gone now.'

'Vincent killed him when he stole our ship.' There's a firmness in Zannah's voice, and her eyes have hardened. Her knuckles show white as she grips her knife. 'I'm going to kill him.'

A silence hangs around the table. Gideon's never seen this in her. He thought he knew her every aspect – and how could he not, having shared every moment of her life? Joshua and Simva are equally perturbed: but it is Gremykoff who breaks the silence before either can speak.

'The commandment is short, my child: *Thou shalt not kill.*'

'But he –'

Gremykoff cuts her off, with a raising of one huge

166

hand. 'Let me tell you a story. That barbera the Aleut gave you. Why stood it empty?'

Zannah frowns. She doesn't know. Her mother's expression shows she doesn't either.

Gremykoff continues. 'It was the house of proud people, kin to Tukum and Attu, who brought you here. Good hunters, born to the kayak and the harpoon. As the fur-traders, the promyshleniki, very well knew. They took hostages, and forced these Aleut to hunt for them, taking many more otters than the Aleut ever would. So when the otters were almost gone, and the Aleut weary of their oppression, they resisted. They fell upon the promyshleniki camp, and drove them off: but not without cost. It is true that the deaths they caused were of men whom few would mourn: but a killing is a killing, and every killing has its consequences.'

Gremykoff spears a chunk of meat with his fork, and holds it over his dumpling, dripping thick brown sauce. 'The consequences for the Aleut were terrible. Children your age drowned; women hauled away as slaves – or worse; and the men, the brave men, butchered, while they tried to fight them off.' He holds Zannah's huge-eyed stare, till she blinks, and her eyes slide away, defeated.

Still Gremykoff goes on. 'The Aleut will not live in

the barbera. They cannot sleep among ghosts.' Gideon shivers. He's not sure *he* can sleep there now. 'And when you first came ashore, that stormy night, they thought *you* were promyshleniki too, come for more killing.' He reaches across to cup Zannah's chin in his hand, and bring her gaze to his again. Her eyes still shine, but the hardness has gone. 'Until of course they saw your face, my child, and knew you as almost one of them.

'If you find your ship, who do you think will pay the price if you attack this man. You? Your family? Or those who brought you ashore, and housed you, and taught you hunting, and gave you use of their kayaks?'

He withdraws his hand. Zannah looks down at her plate. A single tear runs down her cheek and drops into the stew.

'The loss of something loved is always cause for sadness, and when it is not lost but taken, cause for anger too. But if you act on your anger, you become as those who wrong you. There is too much anger in the world for you to add to it.' He pauses and smiles warmly at her. 'Now, child, sup your stew, tears and all, and tell me of your parrot. I have never seen one.'

Zannah only sniffs, but again Gideon rescues her. 'Pirate. He rode our dog like a horse.' He smiles at the memory. 'He could say hello in five languages.'

'And goodbye in six,' says Zannah. 'We've kept some feathers. I'm making a hat to put them on. A kayaker's hat.'

Simva joins in. 'There was something he said often, after we picked up Vincent in the boat. It made Vincent angry. What was it?'

Joshua remembers. 'Poor Michael's last words. *Beware the crow!*'

Gremykoff stiffens, and for the first time his smile falters. He turns to Joshua. 'This Vincent . . . did he – did he have marks about his neck?'

'Not that I saw. He always wore a scarf. Simva?'

'He said he was burned there. He'd let no one see.'

'I saw,' said Gideon. 'That night when Jacques talked of his restaurant. Pirate tugged the scarf aside. It wasn't a burn. I think it was a tattoo.'

Joshua looks directly at Gremykoff. It is his turn now to sound hard and vengeful: 'Who is he?'

Any reply Gremykoff makes is drowned by an eruption of noise behind the door. The low buzz is overwhelmed by a chorus of bells and chimes, some tuneful, others striking the hour, and all in unison marking the passage of time. Gremykoff smiles, as he gets up to open the door, and lets the swelling wave of noise pour into the room. 'My clocks!' he shouts.

Behind the door is a kind of workshop, with a long heavy bench running the length of it. At the far end hammers and saws hang above a half-built chair, amid a pile of sweet-smelling wood shavings. Nearer the door the tools are finer, and pieces of shiny metal are carefully arrayed on tin trays lined with paper. All kinds of clock line the walls, still ticking steadily as the last chimes die away. Gremykoff closes the door on the clocks and all talk of Vincent.

When dinner is done Gremykoff takes the twins into his workshop, and shows them where to hang their hammocks. 'Most guests find the clocks soothing: but if the noise is too great you may sleep under the table,' he reassures them.

Gideon peers at the dismembered clock on the bench, its intricate complexity laid bare to inspection. He's amazed it is possible to build something like this, never mind repair it with nothing more than the delicate tools carefully laid about.

'Your father's countrymen made this one,' says Gremykoff. 'And it is no ordinary clock. Look.' He picks up a watch-maker's eyepiece, and shows Gideon how to screw it into his eye, then guides him close to the body of the clock, its brass and gold and silver enlustred by the dying sun and Gremykoff's candle.

In magnification the mechanism is even more elaborate, an interconnected network of springs and cogs and wheels within wheels. The point of a watch-maker's tool intrudes into Gideon's field of view, held with a remarkable absence of tremor, in Gremykoff's bear-like paw.

'This is the chronometer from the British warship you paddled past. Without it they are lost. They cannot safely navigate the oceans that separate them from their distant home.

'See this?' The very point of the tool rests on a minute spring, which bears a crack. 'This tiny flaw puts the whole mechanism out, and the navigator off course, so that ship and crew are dashed upon the rocks.'

He turns to Zannah. 'Consequences, you see.'

He straightens, lowers the tool, and speaks now to the two of them. 'In every work of man there are flaws, and even the smallest flaws may lead to disaster. You and I are also flawed, but we are not machines – though some say so. For, unlike any clock, we can *know* our flaws. And once they are known we can correct them.'

He raises a hand in a good-night blessing. 'Dosvedanya.'

'Dosvedanya,' Gideon replies

'Spasibo,' whispers Zannah, already in her hammock.

CHAPTER 7
FOG BEASTS!

THUNK! THE SLENDER HARPOON STRIKES the chalk target dead centre. The post shivers, and splinters of rotting grey wood fly off: but the harpoon sticks. The young Aleut girl – Gideon doesn't know her name – smiles at him, then hands over her throwing board and another harpoon. Challenge twinkles in her eye.

Gideon turns the weapons over in his hands. The harpoon is more of a dart, and not at all like the evil-ended nine-foot spears he's seen on the decks of whaling ships. Its three-foot shaft runs from a blade of sharpened bone to the flight of stiffened skua feathers, bearing multicoloured rings along its length. The throwing board is odd: a flat palette of wood, with a hole near halfway and a notch at one end. He tries it various ways, struggling to recall how the girl wielded it. He's seen Tukum and other hunters use just such a board to increase the accuracy and range of their one-handed strikes from the kayak: but here, on land, with both hands free, he cannot figure it out.

The girl laughs at his clumsy incomprehension, before she demonstrates the grip. Gideon nods: *of course!* He presses the end of the dart up against the notch, and pushes his forefinger through the hole to grip the shaft against the board. He turns to face the post – the only upright target within range – and takes aim. It marks the corner of a broken-down fence enclosing a set of low hillocks, much overgrown, at the far end of the village, close to the beach.

Zannah watches the concentration in her brother's face. She's hardly slept, her night disturbed more by the silence from the broken chronometer below her berth than the madly ticking clocks all about. Gremykoff's words – *We are all flawed* – rang in her head every hour.

Gideon launches his harpoon and watches, dismayed, as it flies wildly astray, and soars over the fence to disappear in the long grass beyond. The Aleut girl waves him away, still smiling, and says something he cannot follow. 'You have to fetch it,' says Zannah, coming awake at last. 'If you miss the post you must fetch the arrow, wherever it falls.'

Gideon shrugs, hands the throwing board back, and sets off. Behind him Zannah says something in Aleut. Gideon tries not to hear the giggles: he knows he could never face down two girls who speak a language he does not. He vaults the broken fence.

The grass beyond it is long and untended: finding a harpoon will be hard, however brightly painted it might be. He stands where he thinks he saw it land, and sweeps through the tangled growth with feet and hands. Nothing. *Maybe to the right: I can't have been that far out.* Still nothing – but behind him, more giggles. *Then the left.* No. *Up here, maybe* – and he's on a small summit, where the grass is shorter, and there stand, like low and lonely unleaved trees, scattered wooden crosses. And now he knows the reason for the giggles: he's in a cemetery, hunting among the headstones of the dead for a misfired harpoon.

He decides to ignore the girls further, and looks about. Most of the crosses are of the Russian three-barred type, and bear the same strange Russian lettering he's seen in Gremykoff's church. Many are overrun by grass and some have fallen over. Any paint they bear is cracked and peeled and grey. Here and there stand sporadic crisper crosses, whose still-bright letters Gideon understands no better for their clarity.

He steps towards what seems the newest cross, and strikes his foot on something hard, something hidden under grass, and stumbles, wincing in pain. He kneels to rub his toe, and bends away the tatty fronds that cover an ancient headstone. He scrapes away moss and lichen, and crouches close, to run his hands over letters and words at once familiar yet oddly out of place. A marmot chitters at him, as if to warn him off, but Gideon persists until the inscription is fully visible:

Able Seaman George Wharton, of HMS Resolution.
Born Whitby 28th June 1739.
Died Oonalaschka 6th October 1778.
As near to heaven by sea as by land

Gideon fingers the rough stone, lost in thought. *An English sailor, a hundred years and half the world away from home . . . Such a lonely resting place.*

He's forgotten all about his harpoon: but a sharp bone-blade rap on his head and a fierce shriek in each ear startle him back to the present. He jumps up and whirls round to see Zannah wielding his lost harpoon, and her Aleut friend the throwing board. Both are laughing wildly. Gideon stands aloof and folds his arms, waiting for them to run out of breath. When at last they fall quiet, he indicates the crosses with a sweep of his arm, and admonishes Zannah. 'Show some respect, will you? This is a burial place.'

Zannah's smile subsides. Although she doesn't understand his words, the Aleut girl reads his meaning full well from his tone, and his gestures: she's suddenly subdued too.

Gideon bids them kneel by the headstone, and watches as Zannah reads it. She looks up at him when she's done.

'Yes,' he says. 'Captain Cook's ship. From Captain Cook's town.' Both knew it was also Joshua's town, though he never speaks of it, and has never taken them there. 'He's a long way from home.'

'Maybe he got to like it here too,' Zannah ventures.

'Too?'

'As much as we have.' She sees him frown. 'Well, as much as I have.'

She turns aside and exchanges Aleut words with the girl. Gideon watches, and listens, but takes little in, till Zannah addresses him again. 'Pliktanax – Plikta – says the English spent a month here. Her great grandfather hunted for them. Some call their anchorage English

Bay now. But not her family: to them it is still Samgoonoodha.'

'Well I'll call it English Bay, if ever we're to go there, before we leave.'

'You call it what you like. I'll use its real name, however long we stay here.' Zannah's challenge makes Gideon uncomfortable: but not surprised. He hears it more and more these days. *It's as if she wants to be an Aleut*, he thinks.

She turns back to Plikta, and there's more Aleut, repeated and emphasised with gestures, till Zannah's sure she understands enough to translate. Plikta's eyes are bright with defiance as Zannah speaks for her. 'The Russians were here before the English. The Americans came after. The Aleut – the People – were here when the world began, and will be here when the world ends.' But Zannah's not just translating: she's participating in the sentiment, and angered that her brother is not: *It's as if he's forgotten half of who he is*, she thinks.

Gideon looks away and stands to survey the bay from the vantage point this low cemetery hill affords. Out in the deep water the barques, the brigs, the steamers ride at anchor, the flags of many nations at their sterns. Close inshore, past the end of the beach, a solitary Aleut hunter sits motionless in the aft cockpit of a two seat kayak. The fish spear in his raised right hand jabs downward into the shallow water, and he hauls up a thrashing fish. He pulls it off the spear, and leans forward to drop it into the empty kayak seat in front of him. The fish is lost to view, but droplets of water and sprays of scales flash silver in the sunlight for a time, till the thrashing is done.

The two girls are standing now too, on either side of Gideon, and watching what he watches. 'Yaayaaxs,' says Plikta, proudly. 'Yaayaaxs,' Zannah repeats. 'It means uncle.'

Nearby shouts intrude on the peace. Without so much as a glance over his shoulder to show that he has heard them too, the fisherman paddles off along the shore. More shouts come, louder and clearer, but breathless now, and punctuated by hollow thumping sounds.

Gideon listens, amazed. '*They're English!*' he exclaims. The three of them scramble back over the cemetery fence to see, on the flat patch of grass, a group of husky sailors kick a heavy leather ball about, hampered by clumsy boots and a general absence of talent. Plikta's friends sit on a bank nearby, watching with interest, and Plikta leads the twins across to join them.

'Ye kick about as straight as a puffin flies, ye manky hoofer ye,' bawls a burly figure standing between two poles newly driven into the ground. He kicks the ball back towards the object of his abuse, who immediately falls over. Gideon looks at Zannah, unable to contain a smile. They've kicked enough footballs on enough sunny beaches, and beaten Nathan and Kanaka enough times to relish a challenge renewed. Inside seal-skin boots their feet suddenly itch to run and pass and shoot.

There's a question in Gideon's eyes next time he looks at her: and nothing but a nod in her reply. 'Yes,' she grins. 'Oh yes. But speak only Aleut.'

'I don't.'

'Then make it up.'

A stray pass sends the much-scuffed ball their way. Zannah controls it with one foot and flicks it up in the air with the other, for Gideon to volley back towards the goal. Plikta and her friends applaud with gusto.

"Eyup, Eddie. These Eskimo can play,' says a sailor.

'Fluky as a whale's tail, Billy boy,' shrugs another.

'Let's see, eh?' Billy beckons the twins forward, and passes the ball to Zannah. She dribbles towards him, and just as he lunges at her in a clumsy tackle, she passes to Gideon, who shouts something incomprehensible to Aleut and *kabloonah* alike, and passes the ball back through Eddie's legs.

'I reckon ye've jes' bin nutmegged by a pair o' flukes,

lad,' laughs the big man in goal, as Plikta jumps up in celebration and leads her eager friends on to the pitch.

'And I reckon we've enough for a match now, boys,' says Billy.

'What, us agin them?' Eddie's still dismissive. 'Eskimo chidren?'

Gideon and Zannah exchange some more made-up words, as Eddie approaches, determined to retain the ball and prove a point. A team tackle later he's on his back and dispossessed, and a point is indeed proved, but not the way he wanted.

Before long the pitch is a melee of lumbering English sailors and skippy Aleut children, who run and whirl among them like kayaks through a battle fleet. The hubbub of shouting and laughter attracts others, even more lumbering because they don't know the game, but eager to learn, and equipped with their own goalposts.

'C'mon, you limeys. Try some guys your own size,' jeers an American voice. 'And then we'll play you at *real* football.'

'Ye mean rugby? 'Twas us invented that too, my yankee friend,' replies Eddie, determined to salvage some pride.

But even as the Americans and English line up opposite each other, ignoring the children, Tukum and

Attu and their Oonalashka kin step forward. Tukum grabs the ball as it passes, and waves it first at the white men to one side, and then at Aleut – adults and children alike – on the other. He says nothing, but the challenge is unmistakable. There's a shake of hands, and while the goalposts are set, and the teams arranged, the spectators arrive. Gideon spots Joshua, deep in serious conversation with two men in uniform: the captains of HMS *Greylag* and USS *Bear*, come to see the sport of their crews. He doesn't see Simva till she joins him on the pitch, smiling and telling him, till Zannah shushes her, how she's here to even up the odds. 'Aleut. Speak only Aleut,' Zannah says . . . in Aleut.

A shrill whistle announces that there is even a referee: Gremykoff, who towers above limey and yankee and Aleut alike. He has cast aside his Sunday robes and takes up the ball, whistling furiously till he has everyone's attention, and the banter falls silent. With great ceremony he kicks the ball high in the air, then steps aside as it descends, and the teams close in. Gideon lets out a blood-curdling war cry in no one's language but his own, the ball strikes the turf, and battle is joined.

The game ebbs and flows over the pitch like a turbulent tide, but since most players' enthusiasm greatly outweighs their skill, any goals are few and scrappy. The two Russian drunkards, who'd been penitent and as sober as their clothes were dry that morning in church, pass a bottle back and forth, to punctuate their commentary on the match. One applauds every move and every goal, with shouts of 'Horosho! Horosho!' no matter which side scores; while the other hurls impenetrable Russian curses on the same players for the very same acts, again regardless of which way they are kicking. Neither of them notices that they take such opposite views, they are enjoying themselves so much.

Only the three captains stay serious, as they stand near half-way, barely watching the game. Gideon crosses to patrol the wing nearby, hoping to eavesdrop, as he trots past or pauses to await a pass. Mostly their talk is a low rumble, hard to make out: but one word seems to rise above the others, again and again, distinct and compelling: *gold*!

Eager to hear more, Gideon edges closer, till a look from Joshua and a shout from the pitch draw him away; but only briefly. When, on his next run down the wing another word – *Vincent* – leaps out from the rumble of talk, Gideon hurls himself to the ground, and rolls theatrically over. He sits up straightaway, smiling to show he's unhurt, and waves aside looks of concern from

Joshua and Simva. He slips off one boot and inspects it, as if to blame it for his fall, and then mimes urgent repair work, while suppressing his panting breath, the better to listen.

He's close enough to hear more clearly now, and it's the American, Captain Healy, who speaks. 'Every spring they go North by sea to Nome . . . and then the Yukon. A summer slaving for gold, sustained by dreams of riches: then back here for winter, to lick their wounds and ready up for the following year.'

Joshua's voice is distinct. 'Then he'll return?'

'Be sure of it. But be sure too that you do not steal her back. I am the law here, and I will see no bloodshed.'

Joshua turns to the English captain. 'I am English, as is my ship. She flies the ensign, or did until that damnable pirate took her. You are the English Navy. Will you do your duty by me?'

'My duty is determined by the Admiralty, and not by you, Captain Murphy. If we encounter your stolen vessel on the high seas we will restore her to you, if we can. But we will not seek her out on the ocean; and the inshore waters are rightly the domain of Captain Healy's Bering Sea Patrol.' He pauses for pompous effect. 'And as the local voice of the Crown, I too counsel you against violence in American waters, or on American soil. English you and your ship may be: but your crew, and your – ah – *family* are not. We can offer little enough protection to you, and none at all to your motley band.'

Joshua stares coldly at each man in turn. His voice, when it comes, is tight with controlled anger. 'I will have my ship, sirs, with or without your aid. Mark me, I *will* have my ship.'

The ball smashes into Gideon's side, knocks him over and sends his boot flying. The clumsy sailor who's kicked it – Gideon can't tell if he's English or American – guffaws at him. *Motley band? How dare he?* Gideon thinks as he picks himself up, slips his boot back on, and gathers the ball. As he makes to throw it in his sister sees a familiar set in his jaw. She runs forward to take a pass.

Gideon looks the sailor in the eye, then says in his best Yorkshire accent, loud enough for all three captains – but especially the Englishman – to hear: 'We're going to win the cup!' And he throws the ball to Zannah's feet.

Zannah regards the astonished sailors before her, and grins at the nearest one. 'We're going to win the cup!' she shouts.

Deepening astonishment makes the sailors miss Gideon's run behind their backs; but Zannah spots him, and lifts the ball over their heads. Gideon traps it and dribbles forward. 'Eee!' he yells, passing back to Zannah, who's now on a parallel run close by.

'Aye!' she shouts, and quickly passes the ball back as Gideon nears goal. The goalkeeper's eyes flick between the twins, as they race towards him, shrieking his own football songs in his own distant dialect. He freezes, unsure whether to advance and tackle Gideon, or wait for the pass he'll surely play to Zannah. So he does neither.

Seeing this, Gideon and Zannah raise a combined shout of 'Addiooo!' as Gideon dummies a pass to his sister, then guides the ball past the keeper and into the goal. He and Zannah run past the posts, to cross behind the goalkeeper, where their raise their arms in joint celebration, and turn to race the length of the pitch, voicing again their defiant cry: 'We're going to win the cup!'

The sailors look at each other in disbelief. An American asks Billy: 'What language was that?'

Eddie replies for him. ''T weren't Eskimo, that's fer sure.'

'Aye. And they play Yorkshire too,' Billy mutters.

A whistle from Gremykoff signals the restart, and the match is suddenly more serious. The tackles are harder, the pushing and shoving more vigorous, and the Aleut find themselves floored more often, wincing, and breathless, and bruised. There's a grimness about the sailors now which Simva doesn't like. Gremykoff senses this: he calls a halt and addresses both teams. 'Oddly for me, I have no timepiece to call the game to a halt. The scores are level, so the next goal will win.'

Billy, Eddie and an enormous American launch a driving attack. Their forward surge founders on Attu's athleticism and courage in goal. When he gets up, bleeding from a head wound, he rolls the ball to Gideon, with a mutter Gideon doesn't understand, but a clenched fist and a facial expression he does.

Giddy nods, and sets off on a solo dribble, then exchanges passes with Simva while Zannah slips goalwards, unnoticed. Gideon finds himself penned in at the corner, with ugly sailors bearing down upon him, and no one to pass to. He cannot see his sister, but he does hear her call, high and loud and urgent, from somewhere in front of goal, and he launches the ball.

Zannah's view is blocked by burly backs, till the ball rises above them. She steadies herself as it begins to drop. The sailors in front are each at least a foot taller than her, but she knows she's nimble. She runs at their backs, jumps to place a hand on each shoulder, and hauls herself high above them to meet the falling ball with her head.

The impact is stunning, and hurls her to the ground with a hollow thump that reverberates inside her head. Her senses are scrambled, but she can still see the ball slip past the goalkeeper for the winning score; and still hear the roar of celebration from her Aleut team-mates.

Gremykoff blows his whistle to signal the end of the game, and runs over to Zannah, for fear she might face retribution. But now that the sailors know they are defeated, and are observed by their captains as well as the church, they take it in good heart, and offer handshakes all round.

The captains call their crews away, but they leave the pitch, the goal posts, and the ball to the joyful Aleut, who have already started another game among themselves. The Russian drunkards, whose shouts had grown ever more slurred, lie collapsed in the grass.

Gideon pulls his sister to her feet, and Simva wraps an arm around the shoulders of her twins. Only Joshua stands alone, looking from the football field to the swinging ships in the bay: and only Gideon knows what is on his mind.

The two kayaks ride no lighter on the next day's return journey than they had when outbound, for the provisions they have consumed are replaced by a new cargo of books, charts and tools, as well as spices, salt and pepper, and other foods they cannot find for themselves in their new island home. *I had a ship full of these things once,* Joshua muses. *And now I'm reduced to a pair of borrowed canoes.* His paddles dip and twirl in a smooth procession of strokes. *That villain stole not only my ship, my home, and my livelihood: he took a part of me. If ever he returns he will pay dearly, whatever the words of the Church, the Admiralty, or the US Navy.* He grips his paddles tighter, and the puddles they leave trail behind the kayak in angry swirls. *He will pay.*

Seeing the weather dawn fine, for a rare third day in succession, Tukum and Attu bade them farewell that morning, wishing to remain in Oonalashka a little longer, and happy to let Simva and Joshua find their own way back.

It's been an easy trip so far, with not a breath of wind, nor the merest lift of swell. The sea stretches flat on every point of the compass, a grey-blue skin pocked here and there by sea-birds dropping from the sky, or drifting lazily on the surface like feathered flotsam, too sated by fish feasts to fly.

The sun's still high, but its light is diffused through a shimmered haze, so the shores of Umnak, their home island, some miles ahead, are softened and fuzzy, while far astern Oonalashka lies now completely veiled. Joshua calls a break for refreshment, and now that the paddling's paused, they drink in both silence and water in restorative draughts. It seems wrong to speak and break the spell, so conversation is sparse and whispered. Joshua's happy in his family's togetherness on a day so full of peace, whatever thoughts of retribution he still harbours.

It is Simva who first sees that Umnak's dimmer now. 'Is the tide pushing us back?' she asks.

Joshua stares ahead, and at the water around them, utterly still and untroubled by any tidal swirls. He rummages in his memory for the direction of the tidal set, as plotted on the old Russian charts Gremykoff had given him. 'No,' he says firmly. 'The tide's not running now. It's the haze that's getting thicker. Could be fog coming down.' He corks the water flask and picks up his paddle. 'We need to press on.'

The fog is soon upon them, approaching with a silence and speed that disorientates the mind and chills the body. Joshua only knows that his world of ocean and islands has shrunk to this: two fragile kayaks which bear him, his precious family and a few trinkets.

Gideon looks around, alarmed that he cannot even

see the other kayak now, till an exchange of hoots from Simva behind him, and Joshua, in the other boat, brings them back together. Zannah holds the boats close while Simva unreels a thin rope. She passes one end forward to Gideon, to tie to his bow, and the other across to Joshua to lash to his stern, and in this manner the kayaks are joined.

When the lashings are secured, Simva hands a knife on a lanyard to Gideon, who slings it round his neck. 'We'll tie up in the fog, Giddy, but if there's need you must be ready to cut the line, and to do it quickly.'

Gideon doesn't want to think what might make this necessary, and prefers to concentrate on what he knows now will be his job: to paddle as steadily as he can, and never let his eyes leave the tow-line that stretches in front of him. He must not let it tug, or snag, or loosen.

Joshua points with his paddle to starboard. 'North,' he says instinctively, without hesitation. Gideon regrets that neither he nor his sister inherited their father's compass needle certainty. 'If we paddle west for an hour, then turn south, we should find the end of the island. If we turn too soon, we will miss it, and paddle off into the Pacific. If we turn too late, we'll hit the Northern shore, which we don't know, and we'll be among the rocks. There's no swell, so there'll be no surf to hear.

Listen instead for birds, for people, for grass, for dogs.'
He smiles at Gideon and Zannah in turn. 'Listen for
otters. There will be no talking.'

Simva starts tapping the water with her paddle as
Joshua continues. He joins in. 'We'll paddle slow and
steady, in this rhythm. Listen now,' and the paddles
beat out a pace, like a sleeping heartbeat. 'Zannah, how's
your counting?'

'In English not bad. In Aleut . . . well . . .'

'You'll count in your head. I don't mind what
language, just get it right. Count the portside strokes.
Every sixty makes a minute. Take your little finger off
the paddle, and after a minute swop with the finger
next to it. Call out every time you change your thumb.
Got it?'

'Yes.'

'Giddy – you count her thumbs. When you get to
twelve you call out once. The rest of the time you listen.'

And so they set off, each twin conjuring an image of
the end they fear most. Zannah pictures herself looking
round as the fog lifts, no land in any direction, storm
clouds racing closer, and the water rippled by the first
puffs of rising wind; while Gideon shudders to see, in his
mind's eye, a razor rock slash the thin hide of his kayak,
and water rise around his knees to drag him down

192

through the forests of kelp. Both of them hope Joshua's right about that hour. Simva sees neither picture: for she knows he is, and she knows that by working together, each trusting the other to perform their allotted tasks, they will reach safety.

'Thumb!' cries Zannah, and Gideon whispers 'Six,' to himself. The kayak convoy paddles on in its foggy cocoon, a disorientating blanket of silent grey on all sides. Zannah's too intent on her counting to notice the faint ripples close by to port, but Simva sees them. Before she can point them out they are gone, so quickly she almost doubts they were there. She frowns, and looks about even more intently as she continues her steady rhythm.

The next time the ripples come they're to starboard, and need no pointing out. Wake-like lines spread over the water in a widening V, where the surface is brushed by something moving underneath it. Something big. Something as big, and as hungry, perhaps, as a killer whale. Others call them orcas, as if the softer name might blunt their hideous teeth: but to Zannah, as to the seals, they are always killers.

The paddling falters, the tow-line tugs, and Zannah

nearly loses count. 'Steady!' hisses Joshua. 'You're due another –'

'Thumb!' Zannah calls, quieter than before, but right on cue, now she's composed herself.

'Seven,' Giddy thinks. Like his sister he tries not to look to either side: he's not sure he wants to see what makes these ripples. They appear on either side at intervals, never close enough to upset the kayaks, and always travelling in the same direction. Eight, nine and ten thumbs go by.

It seems an age before Gideon reaches twelve, but he calls it out clearly, startling Zannah who's heard no voice but her own for an hour.

'That's the hour. We turn four points to port now,' says Joshua. But whatever makes the ripples does not heed him, for the moment they turn, a gentle bump against the lead canoe brings them back to their previous course. Joshua tries a second and then a third time, with the same result, then says, 'We do not steer our own course now, it seems. Back to counting, Zannah, that we may gauge our distance.'

Four or five more thumbs go by, then Gideon and the rest become aware there's more than one set of ripples. Zannah tries to swallow, but her fear-parched mouth won't let her. *Not just one killer*, she thinks, with a shiver, *but a whole family of them* . . . Either side of each kayak the ripples appear, more and more often, and with ever-greater vigour, till the top of a huge curved back breaks the water, finless, smooth and mottled grey-green, to surge alongside with what seems an utter absence of effort for something so large. But it is the absence of fins which prompts Zannah's relief, for it proclaims that whatever the creature might be, a killer it is not.

A long powerful puff of air announces this is no fish, either, for like them it breathes air: but nor is it like any whale they have encountered before. Gideon checks his knife. 'Rest easy, Giddy,' Simva tells him. 'I think it means no harm.'

But there's another bump on the boat, this time to starboard, and firmer than before, knocking her round and threatening to roll her over. Together they steady themselves and right the boat with their paddles, but it happens again and again, and now to both boats, always bumping the starboard bow, and nudging them round to port. It's soon impossible to hold a course, and all their skill is required to keep the kayaks upright.

Zannah finally loses all count of her strokes when one of the creatures surfaces right under her bows, lifts the whole front half of her vessel out of the water, slews it round to port, and drops it back into the water. Her heart hammers and she grits her teeth in fear, trying not to picture the huge sea-beast teeth surely destined soon to close on her legs, crunching bone and muscle and seal-skin boots into a hot pink mush.

'It's all right, Zan,' shouts Joshua. 'They're just steering us again.' The tightness in his voice tells of his own concern, however reassuring he tries to sound. 'Turn to port, like they want.'

It takes no second bidding to make the turn, and as soon as the new course is set ('south southwest,' says Joshua instantly) the creatures vanish, as silently as they arrived. It seems only moments before faint shore shadows show through the fog, and Zannah's bow grounds gently on shingle. No sooner has Gideon unlashed the tow-line and run ashore alongside her than a huge foghorn chorus sings out a single mournful note, held low and long, not far off to sea.

Zannah's eyes meet her brother's, both faces lit up by relief, vented fear and delight. '*Now* do you believe us?' she asks Joshua. 'They're the foghorn beasts. We *did* see them that night, Giddy and me, and I'll bet it was from this shore they've just steered us to.'

Simva looks to Joshua, and then from one twin to the other. 'I've always believed you,' she says simply. 'I just didn't want any promyshleniki to hear of them too.

This must be a secret: just us and the Aleut. The Aleut and us.'

'Fine work there, twins,' says Joshua. 'Fine *team*work. Kayaks show that up: you can't pull in opposite directions if you're paddling the same boat.'

CHAPTER 8
THE SUNDERING

'BUT HOW?' ASKS ZANNAH, STANDING OVER a long dead tree trunk, half buried in greying autumn grass. All its bark is long gone, and the wood worn smooth and pale. 'Trees don't grow here.'

Gideon runs his fingers up and down the grain, and recalls the sawing and sanding when the *Unicorn* was under repair. 'It's not from here.' He stands, looking out to sea, and the endless Alaskan forests he knows lie far below the horizon. 'It's driftwood.'

Zannah looks at the beach and the cold grey sea below. 'So high up? No waves could reach this far.'

Gideon shakes his head. 'A tsunami might.'

'A what?' She wonders if he's making it up.

'A tidal wave, from an underwater earthquake. And there's plenty of those round here.'

'I know. I've felt them.' And so she has: few weeks passed without a tremor or two. Mostly they were little more than hiccups, more noticeable at meal times, when they made tiny ripples in any bowls of liquid, and clinked spoons on the rough wooden table: but sometimes they were bigger, and one had been enough to hurl Gideon from his hammock. No matter their magnitude, Scoresby always felt them first, and marked their advent with howls and whines and whimpers. He's howled more often as summer drew to a close, and the days grew rapidly shorter and colder.

But there's no howling today, for he's enjoying a roam with the twins, now that their day's work is done. He leads them in a steady meandering, with pauses here and there to scratch at fox skulls or eagle feathers. He sniffs at the tree trunk, puzzled by the smell and taste of sea-salt ingrained in this misplaced wood, on a treeless slope so far above the sea.

Gideon pats the dog's head. 'Tsunami. It's a Japanese word, but they get them here too. The islands sit on an earthquake zone – *like a string of beads on a broken neck*, Hal told me. That's why the volcano's still puffing away. You might not notice big earthquakes at sea, but they make waves, which get bigger when they come to land. They can be monsters.' He taps the tree trunk, perhaps hurled there by a wall of water a hundred feet high, a force unimaginable on a day of such windless calm. 'This one was.'

'You'll eat no fresher fish that this,' Simva announces to her hungry crew, arrayed around the barbera that evening. Only Hal and Joshua are absent, as she proudly hands around platters loaded with the results of her day's work – first in the kayak, with Nathan, and then at the fire, with Rosa.

'There's so much!' Zannah cries.

'And plenty more for smoking and drying,' adds Nathan, as he tucks in.

Rosa ladles out her sauce, concocted from the berries she's found on the hill, thickened by the seaweed she's gathered from the foreshore, and seasoned with the spices she's salvaged from the *Unicorn*'s stores. It doesn't matter that Zannah's knife is blunt, for the flaky fish flesh drops away from the bones and skin as if never attached. She pours on a dab of Rosa's sauce and scoops up the first rich mouthful. She hums her appreciation, her smiling eyes swinging between Rosa and her mother. ''S excellent,' she says at last, when she's able to speak. 'Really good!'

A chorus of approval rumbles round the barbera, followed by silence but for the chink of spoons upon plates. Tonight at least they won't go hungry, as they do when the fish don't rise, especially now the puffins have gone. Gideon has so far refused to eat the little birds, as his crew-mates did. He likes them, and envied their departure: one day they were about in their usual squawking thousands, raising families in burrows in the ground, like miniature barberas: the next they had simply left, dispersed to roam the oceans for the entire winter. But he knows that if they'd stayed, his hunger would have eventually won and he'd have ended up eating them too.

When the platters are emptied a full-bellied hubbub grows within the barbera, and rises with the wood-smoke up the ladder and out of the roof entrance, masking the silent steps of descending feet.

Only when Hal is at the base of the ladder, and Joshua halfway down, are they noticed. Hal cracks a half-smile with an obvious effort. His face is pale and pinched, his hands are blue, and when he steps forward to the fire his clothing, like his limbs, is stiffened by cold. 'We've smelt that meal for the last three miles,' he says. 'It's what kept us going.'

Joshua joins him by the fire, where he tries, and fails,

to unbutton his jacket with cold-clumsy fingers. 'The coldest paddle yet. Not a breath of wind, the sea flat calm, but cold like . . . cold like . . .'

Simva steps up to help with the jacket. 'Cold like Greenland?'

He nods, and there's a silence. All want to ask the same question. They wait.

'And was there word, in Oonalashka?' Joshua asks it of himself. He looks to Hal and shakes his head. 'The bay is full of ships again, and the town is full of men, heads addled by drink, spouting stories of wealth won and lost.' He sits down beside Hal, almost *in* the fire. 'But of the *Unicorn* – nothing. None have seen her, and many say if she's not back by now she won't get out this winter. The ice is already thickening, though it's only September.'

He looks up, scanning the familiar faces. 'We should never lose hope. If we do not recover her this year, then it will be the next. But we must prepare to winter in.'

There's another silence, as Hal and Joshua attack the steaming fish, and the crew absorb this news. Gideon shivers at the thought: a whole winter of darkness and storm, scratching for food in the short cold days, and huddled in the barbera for the long long nights. He catches Zannah and Simva exchanging secret glances and trying not to smile. He's suddenly burning inside, far though he is from the fire. *How can they want to stay here?* he thinks, as he turns away and scans the barbera. *How can this be enough for them . . . or for anyone?* He stomps off and up the ladder, to look for the southern stars in the icy sky above.

That night, in her barbera alcove, Zannah lies in her hammock, under extra furs to ward off the autumn chill. Her sleep is troubled and fretful, for in her dreams she stands on the barbera roof, looking out to sea, and drawn there, like her family and the Aleut, by a distant roaring noise. Away on the southern horizon a line of white, miles wide and thickening by the second, surges towards shore with terrifying speed. 'Tsunami!' someone shouts, and all around her people turn and begin a confused pell-mell tumble up the hill, racing for high ground as fast as they can. But Zannah is frozen, clamped like a tree to the turf, as if her feet have dug roots into the soil. Her terrified stare is frozen too, fixed on a gigantic figure riding the wall of water as if it is a wavelet: Vincent. He bears a harpoon in one hand, a rifle in the other, and a maniacal grin on his face.

Around him tumble whales, and fog-beasts, and the wreckage of many ships, in a roiling mass of debris and desperation. One ship still floats, but only just. Zannah recognises it at once as the *Unicorn*, and her brother stands alone at the helm. Vincent looms even larger now, a leviathan hundreds of feet high. He flicks the ship aside with a contemptuous hand, so she broaches and her decks are swept clean by the monstrous wave now bearing down on the shore. Zannah cries out.

Below her Scoresby stirs. He stands and stretches to look into the hammock, where he sees her eyes flick back and forth under tremulous eyelids. He lays his head upon her shoulder, so his ear brushes her cheek. When she's settled, he curls up again on the bench beneath, but a little closer now, and keeping one ear cocked and one eye half-open.

In the opposite alcove Gideon watches. He's been roused from dreams of his own by her cry, but has no dog to soothe him back to sleep. He shakes his head, as if to rid himself of his nightmare visions: watching from his storm-tossed ship, as a gigantic Vincent surfs a cliff-high wave into Barbera Bay, pulverising everything and everyone in its path, including his sister. He lies still, and slows his anxious breathing by concentrating on the breath-clouds that hang above his face, and then, when he has calmed, he listens to the deep still silence outside, and wonders why it sounds so muffled. He looks towards the ladder opening in the ceiling. Slowly, gently, silently, motes of diamond dust drift down from the world above, glinting in the lamplight, till they settle, and blacken, and vanish. It's snowing.

Early the next morning Gideon's first up, followed soon after by Zannah and an excitable Scoresby, who scampers in the new snow the way he used to as a puppy. At breakfast, Joshua announces that everyone is to be freed, for that day at least, of the need to hunt, or fish, or prepare the barbera for the long stormy winter ahead. 'There'll be time enough for all that,' he tells them, wearily. 'Enjoy yourselves today, it being a Sunday, and marked by the first snow. It'll soon melt, but there will be more. We'll all have had enough of the stuff in a month or two.'

Scoresby's antics indicate he'll never have enough of it, and he wants to go higher and higher, where the snow lies thick and drifting. After breakfast he drags the twins behind him, sensing somehow that their destination too is *up*: a peak at the eastern end of the island. He doesn't sense that they have different reasons for going there.

After two hours' steady climb, in deepening snow, the twins reach a ridge which runs between two peaks of the mountain. To the left the cliffs drop sheer to the sea, and house seabirds by the thousand, which wheel and glide far below. To the right the ridge slopes away steeply over the mountain's shoulder, to a nearly snowless valley, out of sight of the sea. Zannah looks back at the spidery trail of footsteps that brought them here, until she finds her nerve. She turns, and sinks to her knees, then lies prone in the snow and crawls forward to lie down and look over the very edge of the cliff. She daren't stand up this close: a sudden puff of wind, a slip on the snow, and she'd be gone . . .

She looks along the jagged line of cliffs curving away to the west, to the place where it is broken by a familiar valley coming down to the sea. It ends in a bay which offers the only shelter on the entire Northern shore of Umnak. She squints, searching for something she knows lies below but cannot quite see.

'It's still there!' she cries, pointing for Gideon, who's now stretched out on the snow beside her. Gideon doesn't need to squint, for he's unslung the telescope he's been carrying on a strap round his shoulder. He pulls the battered but still bright brass from its scratched leather housing, and extends it to its full length, then digs his elbows into the snow and sweeps his magnified disc of vision westwards, till he sees clearly what his sister can barely make out.

A solitary kayak rests high on the beach, well clear of the high water mark and the line of driftwood above it, and is lashed down in the lee of a large rock. Each twin claims it as the one they paddled back from Oonalashka, though neither really knows. Its harder-worked companion now rests on the southern shore, near their barbera home, but when the wind blows strongly from the south it has to lie idle, waiting for the waves to subside. On such days the remote Northern shore is sheltered, at least close in, for as long as the williwaws don't blow down from the mountains. Zannah's relieved: hunting and fishing can continue; though at the price of a treck over the snow-bound pass where Vincent had followed them, way back in the spring.

Having checked that the kayak seems secure, Gideon scans the nearby shore. A dark pillar of rock thrusts upwards, as if to pierce his lens with its dagger-like peak. Surf seethes round its base, even on this calm day, and cutting reefs of rock radiate out from it like the points of a compass. Gideon whistles. 'Every time I see that rock, I'm even more amazed we didn't hit it that day in the fog.'

Zannah turns to him. 'The fog-beasts didn't let us. They steered us clear.'

They've hardly spoken of the creatures since that strange encounter and after Simva swore them to solemn secrecy. They hear them though, on quiet fogbound days, or misty hammock-swinging nights: distant sea-beasts voicing mournful calls, full of a yearning ache which each of them felt deeply, but differently. For Gideon it is a longing for the sea, and not just to live by it, but *on* it again, criss-crossing the oceans in a tapestry of travel, a different seascape every day; for Zannah it is a yearning to stay, to build a home somewhere fixed to the land, even – especially – here, on this wild, remote and scattered empire of wind and fog.

Zannah wriggles away from the edge to check on Scoresby. She rolls a snowball down the landward slope and watches him hurtle after it in a tumbling coil of fur and powder. When he scampers back up, dismayed to find no snowball left in his mouth to give her, she grins and rolls another, then turns back to her brother. His telescope's still stuck to his eye, but he's no longer looking down. She watches him scan the horizon away to the northeast, and the approach to Oonalashka.

'What are you looking for?' she asks.

'Ships. A ship. *Our* ship.'

Far down the slope Scoresby barks at the now much bigger snowball. Zannah pays no heed. 'Why?'

Gideon lowers the telescope and turns. 'What?' he frowns.

'What will you do if you see it?'

'Get it – get *her* – back.' He takes up his telescope again. '*When* I see her.'

Zannah shakes her head. 'He won't come back.'

'Of course he will. They all will.'

'They?'

He turns back, glad of a chance to unburden himself at last of the thoughts he's puzzled over in private for so long now. 'The Gold Rushers. I've worked it out.' He sits up and extends a hand in the direction he's been scanning for ships. 'There's gold on the mainland, far up in the North. Father and Nathan came to know that in Sitka: that's why we didn't stay. *Yellow fever*, remember? I asked Father Gremykoff about it. I thought it was some kind of plague, but he said no. *An illness not of the blood but of the soul*, he told me. I didn't know what he meant then, but I do now: gold fever. Greed. We left Sitka before Sven – and who knows who else – could find out: they'd have jumped ship and joined in.'

'And Vincent?'

'Why do you think he was up here? How did he know how to guide us into the bay that night of the storm? He *made* us come here. I'll bet my boots he and Sven broke the rudder to force us to detour north. He wanted our ship the moment he came aboard her. Remember Michael? *Beware the crow*, he said. He wasn't talking about any bird. He was talking about Vincent.'

'So why do they come back?'

'The winter's too harsh over there. They come back to restock, to provision up, to trade: to bank their dust and nuggets. To prepare for the next year. Gold fever has no cure. He'll return, I know it.'

'And then?' Zannah's growing concerned. The sudden chill she feels is not just from the snow.

'We get her back.' He says it as if it will be easy; as if there will not be guns and knives and angry men to confront. 'And we take her South, far away from this . . . this windswept pimple of an island.'

Zannah stands up, suddenly angered. 'I *like* this windswept pimple. I like the pimple people. I like the cold and I like the wind and I like the fog. I feel at home here.'

Now Gideon's standing too, equally angry. 'Well I don't. I never have. My home is the sea. I'm . . . I'm adrift here on land.' His raised voice tears Scoresby away from his battle with a snowdrift: he bounds up the slope and stands between the twins, looking from one to the other.

'What do you think Vincent will do if you get the ship back?' Zannah asks. Gremykoff's admonition still rings in her ears.

'The ship is ours. What he does after we reclaim her is not our concern.'

Zannah's voice is raised now too. 'But it *is*. You saw how he took the Aleut hostages. He'll take more, he'll steal more, he'll kill. Can you leave that behind?'

'When I quit this place . . .' He indicates the island below with a sweep of his arm, telescope extended. 'All I'll leave behind is Pirate's grave.'

Zannah lunges forward to grab the telescope. She wrestles it from his grasp and hurls it over the cliff. They both watch its graceful spiralling fall, till it shatters on the shingle hundreds of feet below.

Scoresby's whine fills the disbelieving silence which follows. He's never seen them like this, and forces his way between them, whimpering and desperately wagging his tail: but all he sees are angry faces and tight clenched fists.

Gideon makes as if to speak, but he's so angry no words will come, just incoherent sounds. He takes a step towards Zannah, hands raised, but he stops himself, fearful of what he might do if he manages to grab her. Instead he races off along the very top of the ridge, sending snow slides down the slope, until he's at the next summit along, where he flings himself full length in the snow, facing East, and shielding his eyes from sun and sister alike.

At first Scoresby follows him, and then, when Zannah doesn't, he turns back and retraces his pawprints to her separate patch of mountain top. When Zannah turns away to head back down, Scoresby's whining reaches a crescendo. His sundered devotion makes him shuttle back and forth between the twins, but never quite reaching either of them. His lifelong loyalty has always been to them both as inseparable halves of a whole. Now, forced to choose, he cannot. With a howl that clutches each twin's heart, he hurtles down the mountain between them, ignoring equally Gideon, on the peak to his left, and Zannah, picking her way down the ridge to his right. Neither can bear to watch him go.

Hal and Kanaka sit on the barbera roof, in what remains of the sun, working on a fishing net they have improvised from unwound twine. Smoke rises from a nearby fire, and drifts upward over racks of drying fish, as if stroking them with ghostly grey fingers, before it disperses in the cold still air. On the shingle above the beach Simva rubs oil into the skin of an upturned kayak. It's so quiet that all three hear Scoresby long before he bursts into the camp, wild-eyed and panting. Hal calls him over and tries to calm him down.

'All alone?' he asks. 'So where's the puppies?'

Simva stands and stares in the direction the dog's come from. Seeing this, Scoresby's whines restart. Simva takes a few steps towards the hill, watching the dog till it is clear he does not want to lead or even to follow her back up the mountain.

She frowns. 'Not good. He never runs off. And whatever's upset him he doesn't want to go back.'

She turns to face the sea, and the faint figures on the distant foreshore, hauling kayaks up the sand in front of the Aleut camp. She waves, then puts a hand to her mouth. 'Nathan!' she shouts. 'Joshua!'

Joshua tugs the leash again, to pull a reluctant Scoresby up the steep slope. 'I don't understand,' he mutters to Hal. 'I've not had to leash him since he was a pup. But if – God forbid – the twins were in some kind of trouble, he'd be hauling *us* up here like a whole pack of sled dogs.'

A piercing whistle sounds from the neighbouring valley. 'Looks like we'll soon find out,' says Hal, as the two men and their hesitant hound all turn to the North, and the valley Simva's searching with Kanaka.

When they crest the separating ridge they see not the two figures they had parted from shortly before, nor four as they hoped; but three. Hal can't tell from this distance which twin it is, but Joshua knows in an instant. 'Zannah,' he says, scanning the valley for her brother. 'But no Gideon.'

Joshua unleashes Scoresby as they draw close. But where the dog would normally bound forward with pounding tail and slobbery jaws, now he hangs back, watchful and uncertain. Zannah's wary too, full of silent tension and none of her smiles.

'Well?' Joshua asks.

'Well what?'

'Your brother – missing. Your dog – distraught. And you – lost.' He stretches out a pause to breaking point. 'An explanation is due.'

Zannah's eyes flit between her father and mother. She tries not to look at her dog. Words fail her. She doesn't want to tell the truth, but the language of deceit is not one she knows. She splutters and stammers. 'We – we – we fell out, Giddy and me. Scoresby didn't like it. I came down alone.' And now defiance flickers in her eye. 'And I'm not lost. I know the way.'

Joshua's response is swift and stern. 'Then you will turn around and show us back up.' He hands her the leash. 'And you will lead your dog.'

Zannah's heard hardness in her father's voice before: but rarely when he is speaking to her. Tears well in her eyes, and she looks away as she takes the leash. Joshua catches her arm, and he crouches beside her. His voice, when it comes again, has softened a touch. 'I care little for the cause of your quarrel; but I do care for its consequences. We are few, and we are far from home –' Joshua bends to reattach the loose end of the rope lead to the dog's collar. While he looks away, Zannah's eyes meet and hold her mother's. There's a barely perceptible slow shake of heads. Both think Joshua doesn't notice as he continues to speak '– and we must not separate. We must bind together like the strands in this rope, making it stronger. Scoresby knows that. So should you. Now take us to your brother.'

Zannah wipes her eyes on her sleeve, and strokes the still uneasy dog. She knows that while he's wrong about being far from home, her father's right about the rest –

she knows without him saying so – but still it's hard to admit. Eventually she raises her hand, and points at the double peak, high on the sky-line. 'There,' she says. 'Right at the top.'

Zannah struggles to hide her rising alarm as she leads the way past the first summit, where she and her brother had fought, towards the next, where he sought refuge. It's already uncomfortably clear to her and her companions that he's not where she said they'd find him, and now the footprints in the snow seem to tell a story she doesn't want to hear.

She stands at the point where Scoresby's pawprints race off down the mountain. Beyond, Gideon's tracks from his angry dash to the second peak are clearly marked: but they are not matched by any that return. Zannah knows that her parents have seen this too. They step carefully along the ridge to the spot where Gideon had flung himself. A deep print of his whole body faces out to sea, with evidence of thawing in the middle. 'He lay here a long time,' says Hal. 'Looking for something, I guess.'

Leading away are more tentative marks, which become recognisable footprints as they stretch towards the North, the edge of the precipice, and a thousand-foot fall.

Zannah falls to her knees beside what look like her brother's last tracks, till Simva hauls her back and tells her not to move. Zannah watches through a film of tears as her mother uncoils the length of light rope she has slung over her shoulder, and ties one end round her waist. She hands the coil to Joshua and Hal. 'Hold me,' she directs them, as she crawls to the very edge of the cliff. Here she lies in the snow, where the wind has carved it into a wavy knife-sharp line. With a hesitation it hurts Zannah to see, she looks from Gideon's one-way tracks, over the edge, to the rocks below. 'Hold tight,' she shouts as she leans over as far as – further than – she dares, scanning the cliffs below for what she most fears to see.

After what feels to Zannah a lifetime, Simva turns and wriggles back from the drop, shaking her head. 'Nothing to see,' she says, flatly. 'We'll need kayaks.'

Zannah's desperate to be useful. 'The Northern kayak's still there. We saw it before we – before we . . .' and she falls silent.

Before what? she asks herself. *Before I saw the last of my brother?* She looks again at his final footprints. *What have I done?* She keeps looking at them to avoid the eyes of her parents, her crew-mates, and even her dog. *What have I done?*

Hal and Joshua race downhill to Barbera Bay in a loping pace that eats up the ground, yet leaves some space for breath. Not that they're using it for talk: Joshua's been silent since the summit, and Hal scarce dares intrude on his thoughts at a time like this.

Eventually he has to say something. 'Don't worry, Joshua,' he pants. 'Between us we'll find him.'

'I'm not worried,' Joshua replies, though his tight face says otherwise. 'I've no doubt that we'll find him. He's half Whitby cliff, half Greenland Alp, and, like his parents, not the type to fall off mountains.'

He's quiet again while they drop into the valley, down to the snow-melt burn. As they splash across he recalls a time when he and Simva did indeed plunge down a mountainside, half a lifetime ago, and half the world away. He doesn't know if Hal's heard this story: though he knows he's seen the scars on his back. They climb up the other side of the valley, and he decides it makes no difference.

'Once. Just once, Simva and I had a tumble when we were very young. But we didn't fall: we *jumped*; and we

218

did it to escape a bear.' They separate briefly, to skirt a boulder, then run on, stride for stride and side by side. 'And most importantly we did it *together*.'

They reach the shore, where they run straight past the barbera to the double kayak hauled up the beach below it. They launch it quickly and smoothly, and within minutes they are in a steady paddle, slipping through the water as rapidly as they'd just raced over the land. It's a mile or more before Joshua speaks again, and when he does it is as if there has been no break.

'So no, I'm not worried. I'm *angry*. I've told them and – I hope – I've showed them, all their lives: when we are so few in the world, we must do what we do together, or we will perish.'

Hal nods, as Joshua, in the seat in front, paddles on, pulling harder now to emphasise his words. 'I learnt this lesson a very hard way. The hardest. But I'll make his, when we find him, and hers, as hard as I must to ensure that they never forget it.'

Hal, matching Joshua's pace, feels the speed of the kayak picking up. 'They already know this, Joshua.'

Joshua shakes his head between paddle strokes. 'Not well enough, they don't. Not yet.'

* * *

Simva and Kanaka have the Northern kayak in the water, ready to launch, when Zannah feels a sudden tug on the lead she still grips tightly in her hand. Scoresby's heard something she cannot, away to the East. She looks about. It's too soon yet for Joshua and Hal to have paddled around in any of the kayaks kept at Barbera Bay. 'Just birds, boy,' she mutters to Scoresby. 'Nothing but birds.'

But the dog's still listening, head cocked. Zannah watches the kayak paddle out into the bay, then turn to the left, blades flashing in a brisk and urgent rhythm. She clambers over the jumbled rocks on the foreshore, watching till the kayak disappears from view, obscured by a huge boulder. She studies the rock, briefly, scanning for footholds, then clambers to the top. As she gets to her feet she hears a bark from Scoresby below, and, simultaneously with it, the noise he's barking at: a strange and tuneless piping, backed by a rhythmic clanking chink. *This is no bird*, she thinks. *And it's coming this way.*

Just offshore the kayak paddles pause, and the little boat turns to face the land: Simva and Kanaka have heard it too. Zannah signals to Scoresby to stop barking, then stares at the buttress of rock between her and this oddly jaunty noise. She waits. Scoresby waits, shivering with tension. Just offshore Simva and Kanaka wait, water dripping from their paddles.

And then, around the rock fall, close to the high water mark, saunters Gideon: whistling absent-mindedly, and cradling a much-dented telescope in his hand.

Zannah scrambles down from her rock, and bounds towards him, screaming.

'I'll kill you!' she shouts, almost incoherent with anger and relief. Behind her Scoresby howls his distress at this conflict renewed. 'I'll kill you for not being dead! How can you be whistling like that?' She batters his shoulders with furious fists, not heeding the shouts from the water to stop. Only the thunk of a hunting dart into the driftwood tree-trunk behind her brings her to a halt.

'Enough!' cries Simva, as she lowers the throwing board, and Kanaka paddles the boat up to the water's edge. 'That's enough!' She leaps from the boat and splashes up to her battling twins, hauling Zannah away and looking to Gideon to account for himself. He brandishes his telescope at his sister. It's badly smashed, and no glass remains. He shakes the telescope case, and its chinking tells how he's spent hours combing the beach for every last fragment he could find.

He looks at his sister coolly when he speaks at last. 'I – I dropped my telescope. A long way. I went down to get it.'

* * *

Joshua is true to his word. In the following weeks the lesson he metes out to the twins is a hard one indeed. If they are to paddle a kayak, or roam the foreshore with Scoresby, or play with the Aleut children, it is to be together. Otherwise they must work, long and hard, and they must always work apart. But the twins have inherited a deep core of stubbornness – and not just from Joshua – so when their working day is done they prefer to mooch about alone than to share with each other what they used to enjoy.

Zannah's fiery fury fades, with the passing weeks, to be replaced by an icy cool between them, a coldness which Gideon reflects back. Scoresby spends all his time now with Hal, or with Kanaka, as the fancy takes him. Today it is Hal, and man and dog pick over the shores of Barbera Bay, searching for shellfish. To the west Zannah scrapes seal-skins with the Aleut women in front of their camp, while in the east, high up on the rocks, a solitary Gideon scans the sea. It is his whistle which signals an unfamiliar arrival. In the Aleut camp, hands set work aside, legs stretch to standing, and heads turn to stare seawards. Today's kayakers are all safely in: what can this be?

Either side of Zannah the Aleut women smile.

'Adang!' they murmur to each other, in tones of welcome. One calls down the barbera ladder. 'Adang!' she shouts, almost laughing. 'Adang!' Then she, her sisters, their menfolk, and a rag-tag band of children and dogs rush down the shore, waving and chattering.

Only then does Zannah see the little flotilla of kayaks, paddling steadily past the pillars of rock that guard the entrance to the bay, and making straight for the shore. She hangs back, puzzling over the word: *adang*. Nearby Hal and the rest of the *Unicorn*'s crew watch and wait, while Gideon scrambles down from his look-out post.

They count four kayaks in all, a single, two doubles, and something they have never seen before: a triple. Oonalashka oarsmen paddle in the cockpits fore and aft, while between them, in the centre cockpit, is an imposing and immediately familiar figure. *Of course*, thinks Zannah. *Adang: father*. For it is Gremykoff, priest, bishop, and father to all the Aleut. He wields no paddle, but sits in splendour in robes and hat and flowing beard, and reads from a text laid out on the deck before him.

As his fleet nears the water's edge his welcoming flock splash out to greet him, and to steady his vessel as he clambers out. There is much greeting, in Aleut and

Russian, when the holy giant steps ashore, and it takes some time before he can break away. He nods to Joshua: 'Dobry Dan, Captain Murphy!'

'Dobry Dan, Father Gremykoff,' replies Joshua, warmly. 'Doing the rounds of your parish?'

'Indeed. Each spring and autumn solstice I visit all the islands. Five hundred miles of babies to baptise, of weddings to conduct, of new boats and barberas to bless. It is my most welcome task.'

He recognises Zannah, dressed head to foot in Aleut clothing and still clutching her seal-skin. 'I took you for a resident, young lady,' he smiles, then looks about. 'But where is your brother?' Gideon steps forward, in his woollen sweater and sailor's jacket. He knows his sister's furs are warmer, but he's making a point, and has been for weeks.

Gremykoff takes in the boy's clothes, and the telescope case slung over his shoulder. 'Like father, like son, I suppose,' he says to Joshua. 'And I'm sure mine is not the vessel either of you wished to see.'

'Is there word?'

'None. Your *Unicorn* is as rarely sighted as the beast she's named after. But most do speak of the hard season they have had. The ice came early, and it seems the gold is gone already.'

Attu calls across, and Gremykoff turns back to his Aleut congregation. 'Forgive me. I have duties.' Tukum approaches to take his place, indicating with one hand the fish racks, already being stripped, and miming with the other the act of eating. He speaks to Zannah and Simva in Aleut, and then, with a twinkle in his eye, to Joshua, in English. 'Dinner! You come!'

Tukum's barbera is crammed. Gremykoff has the seat of honour, where he is flanked by Tukum and Attu. Joshua, Simva, and the *Unicorn* crew squeeze in amongst the Aleut and the Oonalashka visitors, as the food – mussels, salmon, seal meat – is passed around. There is not space enough for everyone, so Gideon, Zannah and the Aleut children take turns on the barbera roof. Gideon and Zannah are never above or below together. They pass in awkward silence on the log ladder as Gideon's full plate goes up and Zannah's empty one down.

Gideon settles on the roof's thin grass. On the thicker grass nearby Scoresby slouches among the Aleut dogs, each worrying away at a walrus bone, but always with one eye on would-be bone thieves. Scoresby's bigger than the Aleut dogs, but they are tougher and wilier. Appropriate dog distances are maintained by low growls and teeth-baring lip curls. Gideon watches, as his own plate is cleared. *Is it like that with me and Zannah now?* he asks himself. *Will it always be?* And he steps towards the ladder.

He descends to a sudden lull in the conversation, and the chinking in his telescope case announces his arrival to the diners below. Gremykoff looks up. 'An unhealthy sound for a telescope, Midshipman Murphy.' He extends an arm. 'May I see?'

Gideon steps forward over the tangle of legs, unslings the case, and hands it over. 'There was an . . . accident,' he says, trying not to look at his sister crouched nearby. 'I carry all the pieces with me, to ensure I lose none. I've reshaped the brass, and gathered the glass, but as yet I have no glue –'

'Not for want of trying, Father,' chaffs Nathan. 'He daily boils bones and seaweed, and with the sticky stinky mess he makes, he tries to bind pebbles together.'

Gremykoff shakes the case. The barbera audience laugh at the rattle it makes. He hands it back to Gideon. 'And what would you see with your . . . your . . . kaleidoscope, eh?'

'Only one thing, Father. The *Unicorn*. My home.' He glances at Joshua. 'Our home.'

Gremykoff looks from father to son; from Joshua, whose face gives nothing away, to Gideon, whose singular purpose is evident to all. 'Hmmm,' he ponders, then turns aside to rummage in one of the bags he brought ashore. No one else speaks until his 'Aha!': and he fishes out a foot-long spyglass of sturdy elegance. It gleams in the dim light, and bears Russian lettering along its side.

Gremykoff extends it to its full length, then holds it to his eye and points it at Gideon. 'What do I see?'

Gideon's puzzled. 'Why you – you see – me.'

'No. I do not. I see a boy who is blind. He sees nothing but what he wants to see, and since what he wants does not appear, he sees nothing. He is blind.' He lowers the spyglass, but still fixes Gideon with a stare like a harpoon. 'He does not see the places or the people around him, for he chooses not to. He does not see the eagles in the sky, the flowers underfoot, or the foxes on the foreshore. His is a wilful blindness: the worst kind.'

He holds the telescope out towards Gideon. 'I will lend you this, my young look-out; and when in a few days I return this way, I will reclaim it from you.' Gideon takes hold of the telescope, though Gremykoff will not release it from his grasp, or Gideon from his gaze. 'But heed me, and ask yourself this: why do I lend a precious instrument

227

of vision to a boy who is blind?' Gideon can't tell if he is supposed to answer, so he stays silent, conscious he is watched by everyone in the barbera, and every one of them has heard these words of admonition. He can do nothing but stare mutely at the priest until he is released. Gremykoff stretches the silence, then lets go at last of the spyglass. 'Open your eyes, boy, and open your heart.'

Gideon mumbles his gratitude, as he tucks the surprisingly delicate instrument into an inner pocket. He fingers the straps on his own telescope case, and asks, tentatively, 'Shall we swop, Father?'

'No, no, no!' cries Gremykoff, with a laugh. 'How many fish shall we catch if our kayak rattles so?' Laughter rises from the English speakers, and then, as Simva translates, from the Aleut, until Gideon begins to blush. Gremykoff chooses the moment to relent. 'If you see better when next we meet, I will carry your kaleidoscope back to my workshop, and see if I can repair it.' Gideon blushes ever deeper red. He backs away, nodding thanks, towards the ladder, where he clambers up to the sky-space above. Zannah follows, soon after.

She's halfway up the ladder when she sees him snap open Gremykoff's spyglass. He brings it to bear at once on the peak where they had parted in anger. 'I see a mountain,' he says, to no one in particular. He swings it round to Scoresby, slobbering over a walrus bone: 'I see a monstrous hound, devouring a whale.' And now, noticing Zannah emerge from the barbera, in full furs, with seal-grease round her mouth, and a bone knife in her hand, he turns his gaze to her. There's a pause, before he speaks again, more quietly now: 'I see a native. It doesn't look hostile, but you never know.' And he strides away.

Gideon stands up stiffly next to the pile of carefully knotted fishhooks he's been working at all morning. 'I'm finished,' he calls to his mother. 'Can I go now?' He knows his father wouldn't let him: but Joshua's out at sea.

Simva comes over. She's anticipated this, and knows it's better to let him go, but limit his range, than confine him to the camp. 'A good day's work, Giddy: so yes, you may go. But promise me this. One – you must be back by dark.' Gideon nods agreement. 'Two – you must not go above the snow-line.'

Gideon frowns. 'If I cannot go over the snow-line I cannot cross the pass. You may as well keep me here.'

Simva ponders. 'All right. Above the snow-line only

229

to cross the pass. No teetering over precipices, understand? Remember we can track you, if you do. I might just follow you myself.'

Gideon picks up his food pouch and makes as if to leave; but Simva hasn't finished. She indicates a bundle of furs. 'And three – you must wear proper clothing. We do not need to see your seaboots to know you would be a sailor again.'

Now it's Gideon's turn to ponder, as Simva unfolds the anorak he's not worn since that day on the mountain top. He slips off his tattered woollen sweater, and pulls the windproof garment over his head.

Simva pins him half in and half out of his fur. 'If we have to search for you again, then I, as much as your father, will keep you in camp the entire winter, Gideon. Understand?'

'I understand,' he replies gravely, not voicing his thought: *but we won't be staying that long*. And once fully furred, with Gremykoff's spyglass slung over one shoulder, and his food pouch over the other, he sets off uphill. If he looks back he'll see his dog and sister follow him with silent stares: but he doesn't.

He spends the steady and now very familiar climb up to the pass, recalling the first time he'd come this way, and the sight he and Zannah had witnessed that foggy spring night. He still knows little about the fog-beasts, for the Aleut say nothing, not even to Simva, and no one else knows. *No one?* he asks himself. *Maybe Vincent saw them too.* He dismisses the thought. *His head's too full of gold to pay them any heed.*

The snow-line is lower, as he's told his mother, and the ascent to the summit ridge more difficult than he thought. He's blowing hard by the time he reaches the top, but his breathing halts and his racing heart falters when he looks down to the North Bay far below: for there's a ship at anchor there, and he needs no telescope to tell she's the *Unicorn*.

He jumps back behind the ridge, lest he's silhouetted against the skyline. *I knew it!* he breathes. *I knew he'd come back!* And he hurtles down the snow slope, an avalanche of vindication.

He's not gone far before he's halted by thoughts racing ahead of him. *Stop! Wait. Think. You never thought he'd come back* here, *to Umnak, did you?* He sits down in the snow. *What will they ask when I get to the barbera? What's he doing? What does he want? How many does he have with him? What boats? What weapons?*

He looks at the ant-like figures by the barbera far below, and the smoke curling up from the curing fires. *Who better to find out than a boy with a telescope? And when I go back to tell them all this, they'll have to let me join in the raid to recover her.* And he turns upwards again. *Then everything will be all right again.*

Back at the top of the ridge he packs snow around the telescope to shield any giveaway reflections, and he studies the ship he knows so well. Magnified in his circle of vision, she shows the battering she's taken in Vincent's hands. She's scuffed and scratched and scruffy, and Vincent's foremast repair is a hurriedly bodged job; but she's still the *Unicorn*, his *Unicorn*, and Gideon's heart leaps to see her again, so close at hand.

There's no one about on the ship, but there is a curious cage on the foredeck that is both new and old. Gideon scratches his head, before he recalls the pen they used in the Southern seas, to take livestock from island to island. They had dismantled it on their passage north. It had once housed goats and sheep and pigs, but now its lid is open, and it stands empty. Gideon rubs his eyes, wondering if she's returned as a ghost ship, sailed by phantom sailors and carrying ghost goats and spectral sheep, when a shot sounds. But it is not from the ship.

Some way north a speck emerges from an offshore fog bank, and then another, and another. Gideon fiddles with the focus on the spyglass, and sweeps it round. He freezes at the sight of Vincent in the lead boat, his rifle raised. A puff comes from its muzzle, followed moments later by the distant pop of its report.

Suddenly there is life on the deck of the ship, as sundry sailors tumble up from the fo'c's'le in response to Vincent's signal. They set to work, hurriedly laying out chains and hooks and ropes and pulleys. Gideon shudders at the foot-long knives on harpoon shafts they place on deck, ready for some hideous purpose.

He swings his view back to the approaching boats, and now sees why their progress is slow, for all their urgent rowing. Towed between them, by the tail, is a huge creature, leaking a wake of bright blood, and slowly but steadily sinking in the chilly water. Vincent shouts to the oarsmen in his own boat and the others, then takes up an oar himself, urging them on to secure their catch before it can sink, and the sea reclaim it.

Gideon remembers his father's tales of the terrible whaling trade; but as he looks and listens he learns that this is no whale, and it is not yet dead. For a weak but unmistakable foghorn cry rises in the air. Its drawn-out call ends in a bubbling bleat, soon drowned by crude cries of triumph as it is secured on the *Unicorn*'s starboard side. Now the men in the boats set about the poor creature again with their killing lances, until Gideon, sick to the stomach, has to lower his glass.

He cannot watch as the butchery begins, and the carcass is hacked into pieces to be hauled up on to the deck. He's thankful that the fog bank's closing in, and that, though he listens hard, no other fog-calls come from any companions of the dead beast.

His anger will not let him return to the barbera; not yet. *We owe our lives to those creatures*, he tells himself, looking at the rock needle the fog-beasts steered them past, back in the summer. *I cannot turn away now.* He is instead spurred on, to get closer, to find out more, to ready himself for the fight that must follow, and to do anything possible to prevent any more such slaughter. *Just don't get caught*, he resolves. Once the fog thickens round the ship, and rises to his ridge, he descends, as fast as he can. He detours east to ensure the kayak is still present and hidden from view, and then, more slowly and carefully, he crawls through long fog-shrouded grass, ever closer to the anchorage.

He stops, every few yards, to listen, but the voices from the vessel remain indistinct. He hears Vincent, he's sure, and maybe Sven, but mostly they are gruff men he does not know, excited by their hunt, and their rum, and laughing loud and long.

Gideon crawls closer still, but next time he stops to listen, it is to hear with horror, amid the voices, the creak of oars, and the ripple of a bow wave, and the crunch of a keel upon sand, as a ship's boat comes ashore behind him, cutting off his return route.

He hears two, maybe three men step out, and roll a heavy barrel along the shore, in his direction. He looks about for an escape route, or more shelter, and grows increasingly frantic when he finds neither.

'Not much oil in them beasts,' says one of the men.

'Quality's good, though. An' they're easy enough to catch,' says a second.

'Aye,' cackles a third. 'Just ship oars in the fog, an' go callin'.' They all laugh.

'I reckon a few weeks o' this an' we'll make more'n a whole summer o' futile pannin' fer gold.'

They're coming ever closer, forcing Gideon to make a desperate choice: stay and hide, and hope they don't stumble over him; or up and run, and hope they can't catch up. A thinning in the fog forces the choice upon him, and he scrambles to his feet and up the steep slope as fast as the rough ground and the slippery grass will allow.

They spot him straight away. 'Hey!' comes the shout from the beach. 'An Eskimo!'

Gideon doesn't dare look back. A shot cracks the still air, forcing him upwards faster still, but now in a desperate zig-zag. *If you hear the shot*, Hal told him once, *you're OK.* He hears the next one too, and a whizzing hiss and soft thump to his left. *Zig!* he tells himself. *Now zag!*

He doesn't hear the third shot, but is hurled abruptly upwards and forwards by a kick in his leg as if from an angry mule. He tries to steady himself again, but his leg won't work, and his blood makes the grass slippery. He falls to the ground, surprised there's no pain, and tumbles back down the steep slope, to lie breathless and broken, at the feet of his hunters.

The one with the gun leers down at him as the pain hits. The force of it makes him cry out. 'Well well. A fog-beast and an Eskimo all in one day, eh?'

'Any more of 'em?'

'I'll look around.' As he strides off, the other sailors each grab one of Gideon's arms, and between them they drag him along the beach, smearing his blood over the stones. The last thing Gideon senses, before passing out, is being pitched into the bilge of the boat, to lie among the water barrels. And the last thing he thinks, before thinking stops, is: *I've failed.*

CHAPTER 9
RETURN TO BATTLE

ZANNAH LACKS THE WORDS TO ASK WHAT her Aleut companions want the seaweed for, and why it has to be this particular kind, so she resolves to help them gather it, and then to watch how they handle the bundles of half-dried red-brown fronds. She steps over a tangle of driftwood, and is hit in the right leg by a powerful blow, which sends her a-sprawl on the shingle, where she lies wincing with pain and with puzzlement, for there's no one close by, and nothing's been thrown. *A creature in the driftwood?* she wonders; but there's no bite marks on her furs, or her skin underneath, and neither she nor the Aleut girls now standing over her saw anything.

A pulled muscle? Zannah thinks, as she gets gingerly to her feet. *Can't be: feels fine now.* She indicates to the

Aleut that she's all right, and had simply tripped over the claw-like branches of a washed-up log. The two girls laugh when they see she's still clutching her seaweed bundle, and she guesses from their giggles and gestures that the seaweed's used in a remedy for cuts and bruises; yet here she is falling over while collecting it.

All chatter halts at the sound of a shout offshore: a man's shout, in Aleut, urgent and repeated. Zannah takes a moment longer than her companions to locate its source: a double kayak, paddling in at speed. More shouts, and the precious seaweed is cast aside as the Aleut girls turn and run to their barberas, motioning Zannah to do the same, with a word she knows all too well: 'Promyshleniki!'

When they reach the Aleut village Tukum and Attu are already out of their kayak, and talking intensely to their kinsfolk. Simva, the first of the *Unicorn*ers to arrive, listens carefully, and turns to Joshua and Hal as they draw up.

Joshua looks to her for a translation, but he can tell from her face it is not news she wants to pass on. 'Vincent's back,' she says. 'He's anchored in the North Bay.' She reaches out to lay a hand on Zannah's shoulder. 'He's hunting the fog-beasts.'

'No!' cries Zannah, suddenly understanding the

anger written on the faces of the Aleut around her and the agitation in their movement, as they make hurried preparations to leave. She looks to her father, her eyes drawn by his stillness in the turmoil, as if he is the axis, the pole, around which everyone else revolves.

There's a sternness of purpose in his face, and a quiet force in his voice when he speaks, through Simva, to Tukum. Any celebration of the return of his ship is masked by grim awareness of what it may take to recover her, and a steely determination to do it, nonetheless.

'I want my ship back,' he tells Tukum: but he's talking to them all. 'You want your kin, the hostages he took. We *all* want him away from here, or dead in the fleeing. We will have to fight him, and now we must make ready.' Tukum nods gravely in agreement, and there is a rapid tallying of kayaks, and kayakers, and weapons.

Zannah listens in desperate hope as Aleut paddlers and *Unicorn* crew are assigned to boats; but her name doesn't come, and she turns away disheartened. Simva's prepared for this. 'There will be dangers we cannot let you share, Zan.'

'But to sit and wait here will be torture.'

'I know.'

'So let me do something.'

Simva looks around and sees Hal tying Scoresby to

a fish-rack. The dog watches as he steps into the bow seat of Kanaka's kayak, as if he wants to get in too.

Simva turns back to Zannah. 'Take Scoresby and bring your brother down off the hill.'

'But –'

'He may have seen the ship too, and I want him back here.'

Zannah sees her mother will not relent, so she unties the dog, and as the kayaks continue to launch, she takes him along the shore to her barbera, where she rummages in Gideon's alcove for the jersey he's tossed there earlier. She brings it up to the roof and holds it under Scoresby's nose, calling Gideon's name, and pointing at the mountain. It takes some time before Scoresby understands – he's not played this game in ages – but a sudden urgency has him head off uphill, tugging her after. She has time for one last look at the fragile fleet of kayaks paddling fast towards the island's eastern shore, but as she turns back the pain slices into her leg again. This time she doesn't fall, and she doesn't need to look about to know there's nothing nearby to have caused it. For she remembers, a long time ago, on a sunny shore, Gideon telling her, that when she'd been knocked to the ground by a falling coconut, he had felt the pain too. Now she understands. She unleashes an impatient Scoresby. 'Come on, boy,' she tells him. 'Gideon's in trouble.'

'Aaargh!' Pain yelps Gideon conscious again. He tries to kick out at the monster biting his leg, but his feeble sweep is easily fended off by the other monster, the one on his left. He fights to loose his fists, but finds his hands bound behind his back, and the more he struggles, the more the cords dig into his wrists. The leg-monster bites again, deeper this time, but, in the midst of his agony, something tells Gideon that while he might cry out, it must not be in English. He's pretty sure he's on the deck of the *Unicorn*, where he clings to the hope that he's not been recognised, and Vincent and Sven have dismissed him as just another Eskimo. He's dimly aware of other figures somewhere nearby, and wonders whether Vincent is among them.

Whoever is on his left seems kind. He runs a rough hand over Gideon's brow, drops water into his mouth, and utters soothing words. In *Aleut*! Gideon's eyes snap open. He looks to his left and then to his leg. *Not monsters but men. Aleut men*, he thinks, racking his memory for some Aleut words to reply with. He's too troubled by what's happening to his leg to find any, especially when the man-monster working there digs deeper and harder than ever, while his colleague stifles Gideon's groans.

Then, suddenly, it stops, and there's a grunt of satisfaction somewhere near his knee. Gideon senses a loosening of a tight band round his leg, a warm wetness, and then a calming pressure. The other Aleut shows his face at last, and then his blood-smeared hands. One grips a bone knife, and in the other, between thumb and forefinger, is an irregular metal ball, held up like a trophy. The smiling surgeon grasps Gideon's hand, presses the sticky ball into his palm, and curls his fingers tight around it, with a word Gideon can't catch before he faints again.

'I can't work it out,' Zannah tells Scoresby, as they stare at the snow-marks, high on the ridge of the pass. 'He comes up . . . here. Something makes him jump back . . . just here. Then he turns and runs hard downhill, but suddenly stops, turns and goes slowly back up. He lies down – right here, at the very top – and then he goes down the other side.'

She stares down both valleys, north and south, but all she sees is swirling fog. 'What did he see?

And why didn't he come back? Was he going to take the ship himself?'

A foghorn call, long and low, and even more plaintive than usual, rolls up the valley. 'Maybe he didn't need to *see* anything, Scoresby. Maybe hearing that is enough. It's enough for me.' And she strides out, beside Gideon's downward footprints.

Attu calls a halt to all paddling and cups a hand to his ear. The kayakers all listen intently, glad of a chance to catch their breath. At first there is nothing above the drip of water from their paddles, the scush of waves on the shingle shore, and the cries of sea-birds overhead, but then it comes again: a foghorn, distant, faint, but definite, and one by one they nod. Without a word paddles ply once more, even harder now.

Joshua shouts across to Hal. 'We don't need to hurry. When he hears that, he'll lower the boats and go hunting again. It'll be easy to take the ship when she's crewless.'

Simva turns in the bow seat ahead of Joshua. Her paddle catches the surface and a whisk of spray flies across his face. He blinks the salt water away as she urges him on. 'We *do* have to hurry, if we're to stop him taking any more beasts. We owe it to them.' She gestures to the Aleut paddlers on either side. 'And to them.'

Gideon's woken again, not by pain this time, but by the same foghorn call. And then he is snapped to full alertness by a voice he knows all too well: Vincent, prowling the deck nearby. 'Hear that, men?' he asks. 'Have any of you ever heard money call like that? *Here I am*, it says. *I'm wealth, and freedom, and ease. Come and get me.* All you need is a harpoon and the will to wield it, eh, Sven?'

Sven. That turncoat. That Judas. Gideon squeezes his bullet till it bites his fingers, and keeps his eyes tight shut, afraid of what he might do if he sees the big Swede's face.

But he cannot shut out his voice. And now words come more freely than ever they did before. 'The longer we stay the more we risk discovery. Captain Murphy –'

'*Captain* Murphy? *Captain?*' Vincent's sneer sounds as thick as the skid-grease he'd used to float this stolen ship. 'A man can be no captain when he has no ship, sir! Hang him! He's marooned on this God-bereft rock with his Eskimo spouse and his Eskimo spawn – hang them too! – and he is no threat to us at all.'

Gideon lies perfectly still, in mimicry of sleep, or of death, though Vincent's words live in his ears, goading him to a response. *Later*, he tells himself. *My time will come.*

'And speaking of Eskimo . . . Back in the cage, you monkey.' Vincent kicks out at Gideon's surgeon and pushes him towards the livestock pen on the foredeck. 'And take this mini-monkey with you.' He kicks Gideon in the ribs. Gideon grunts, and grips his bullet, and bites his lip. *Not recognised*, he thinks, as he is lifted like a folded sail, and flung into the pig pen. His surgeon steps in after him, and is battered into crouching as the latticed lid is slammed shut over his head. Gideon watches the suppressed seething in his surgeon's eyes, as the crew take to the boats, the other Aleut among them. Then he understands: he and his companion in this pigpen are now hostages among hostages, to make the Aleut ply the boats in pursuit of the sacred fog-beasts, and ensure the crew return to the ship with their groaning haul.

Zannah needs no dog to track her brother as far as the snow-line, for his footsteps are planted deep, and his course trends directly downhill. Once the snow gives way to grass she turns again to Scoresby, reminding him of the scent to seek with a fragment of Gideon's jersey held under his nose. He continues straight down for a while, until they are low enough to hear the sea, though thick fog obscures everything but the grass underfoot.

Then, all of a sudden, Scoresby veers off to the right, the east, and tugs a puzzled Zannah after him. Only when they reach the shore, and she sees the kayak, does she understand: but here her frown deepens, for the kayak is unused. The trail leads now to the west, in the grass just above the shingle, and here, above the surf, Zannah hears the sounds of a ship close by: low voices, the bump of wood against wood, the creaking of ropes.

Then comes a sound to chill her bones. 'Lower the boats!' shouts Vincent. Zannah sprawls in the grass, clutching Scoresby close. She listens, trying to count the boats as they are lowered into the water. *Three*, she thinks, *maybe four*.

'Pull away, men, pull away,' calls Vincent, over the dip of oars, in a voice full of cruel greed. 'A few more of these beasts, and we sail south to California, our hold brimful of oil, and our pockets soon bulging with dollars. So pull.' There's a blow, and a grunt, and the voice comes back in a shout. 'You as well, you Eskimo ape! Pull as if it's the last thing you'll do.' A bell rings out from the stern of the ship. 'Which of course it will be.' Crude laughter bubbles up from the boats, as Vincent shouts up to the ship. 'Keep ringing that bell, Mister Blunt. We must find you when we return.'

The fog-damp on the grass chills Zannah's body, but not as much as Vincent's words chill her soul. *He's going to use the Aleut to hunt the fog-beasts – and then he's going to kill them too*, she thinks, still struggling to believe it. *We must stop him. But first we must find Gideon.* When she's sure the boats are well away, she urges Scoresby on, keeping him on a tight leash. He's not gone far before he bends to sniff at something gleaming in the grass. The *Unicorn*'s bell rings again. Zannah parts the thick grass, almost reluctantly, and her breath catches when she sees Gideon's – Gremykoff's – telescope, its strap broken, and its casing smeared with blood. Scoresby looks up at her, and then goes on to the shingle. She holds him back, lest he alert Bellman Blunt, but she's seen enough. There are splashes of blood on the shingle, and a keel-groove where a ship's boat has grounded. Zannah ties the broken ends of the telescope strap together, and slings it over her shoulder. *He's on the ship*, she hisses to her dog, and leads him stealthily back to the kayak.

She checks the upturned hull once more, then unties the lashings, and rolls the boat over. A paddle and a short harpoon are still lashed to the deck, exactly as they have been left. She turns to Scoresby, whose apprehension grows as she ties a line to his collar, and makes the other end fast round a rock, tying him where the boat had been. He watches her anxiously as she lifts the boat – again amazed at its lightness – and steps cautiously on to the shingle. With each passing step she senses gathering restlessness behind her, and her hushing gestures go unheeded. When the fog obscures Scoresby from her view – and therefore she from his – he sets up a rising whine, and she's soon forced to relent. She lowers the boat to the stones, and turns back to fetch him.

It's tricky now, grappling with a kayak, a paddle, and a recalcitrant dog, and trying to do it all quietly, but Zannah edges towards, and then into, the freezing water. As soon as the kayak's afloat she lifts Scoresby into the bow seat, and then, stabilising the kayak with her paddle, she slips into the after cockpit behind him, and pushes off in the direction of the bell.

She becomes aware of a looming bulk, ahead and above, and waits for the bell to sound again, listening meanwhile to the occasional creak of rope, and the lap of water against the hull; the sounds of a resting ship she'd lived with so long but never really heard before.

Directly above her the bell rings out, its echoes hanging in the woolly air, and as they die away she paddles towards where she now knows the anchor chain will be.

It suddenly rears up out of the gloom, weed-trailed and rusty. It misses Scoresby, but Zannah, sitting higher, shudders as cold salty fingers of kelp play across her cheek. She grasps the anchor chain and quickly makes fast. She secures the paddle and unlashes the harpoon, then takes it between her teeth. She reaches up to the slimy chain, and hooks one leg over it, but leaves the other in the kayak, to steady it till the bell comes again.

At the next toll she swings up on to the chain and scuttles up as many links as she can before silence settles. Two or three more bell-covered scrambles bring her close to the top, where she scans both the bowrail and her memory for the layout of handholds. *Next bell*, she tells herself.

But instead of a bell from the stern, there's a bark from Scoresby. There's a moment of stunned silence, then a shout from the stern, and the clump of heavy feet on deck. *Up!* Zannah wills herself. *No good hanging here!*

She scrambles the last few feet, cutting her hands on the flaking rust, and bruising her knee when her foot slips off: but she's up, and she's over, and now she's on deck.

Blunt darts forward from the stern, a cruel blade glinting in his hand. Zannah knows, by some deep instinct, that she must attack him, as the best form of defence, if she's to stand any chance. She whips the harpoon from her mouth and lets out the shriek of an outraged banshee, hurtling towards him along the deck.

Blunt hesitates a moment, then opts to hold his ground, and use his knife to parry her furious charge. An instant before she strikes, there's a sudden row from the pigpen. Blunt is distracted: only for a moment, but long enough for Zannah. Her harpoon drives into the muscle of his shoulder, and his knife clatters to the deck. Zannah kicks it away, and draws back her harpoon to strike again. When he sees this, and the vengeful fierceness in her eyes, Blunt runs. He races to the stern rail, which he clears in a single bound. There's a splash, and a shriek, as the cold water clamps his chest, followed by floundering noises, moving up towards the bows. Zannah looks over the rail, to see nothing but fog. She hears a furious barking which tells her Scoresby's guarding the kayak and the anchor chain, and there's no way Blunt can get back on board. The last she hears is the puffing splash of a poor swimmer as he thrashes towards the shore.

Zannah's already searching the deck for more crew,

her bloody harpoon extended before her. 'It's all right,' says a voice from the livestock cage. 'They left just him to guard the ship. Get us out!'

Zannah retrieves Blunt's knife and hacks at the bindings on the pig-pen lid, till they fall away in stringy shards. Gideon's surgeon pushes up from below, the last tie is severed, and the lid flies open. He leaps out, and embraces her, with a torrent of Aleut. She hands him the knife, and he heads for the stern as Zannah stoops to her brother.

'Took your time,' he says, with as much nonchalance as he can muster.

Zannah doesn't rise to it. 'Is this what you call reclaiming your ship? Crammed in a pigpen, waiting for rescue?'

Seeing that Gideon makes no effort to rise up, she remembers the thumping pain in her leg, and looks down. Exactly where she'd felt the sudden blow there's a neat round hole in Gideon's fur, with a blood-stain radiating out from it. He follows her gaze. 'It hurts. I think they missed the bone, so it should be all right. I can move around but I can't stand on it.' He hands her the bullet. 'Here. This is what hit you.'

She helps him struggle over the lip of the pen. 'Let's get you out this pigpen, before Vincent comes back to make bacon of you.' She's shocked by how pale he looks, and the way he slumps to the deck when she stops supporting him: but he's still thinking ahead. 'Best still ring the bell. If they haven't heard your shrieking, or that boat-dog of yours, they'll be listening for it: you know the way bell-tolls carry in the fog.'

Zannah runs to the stern and rings the bell, struggling to recall how long Blunt rang it for, and how hard, and in what rhythm. She returns to the bow where she rummages in the fo'c's'le locker for a sling and a length of rope. She turns to Gideon, who is looking about the deck of his ship, so familiar, yet so long unseen. Zannah hands him one end of the rope. 'Make that fast,' she tells him, 'and loop two turns round the capstan.' She disappears back over the rail with the sling round her neck and the other end of the rope tied round her waist.

'Where are you going?' Gideon calls after her.

'Fishing,' she yells up to him, from halfway down the anchor chain. 'For dog-fish.'

She hangs from the chain, right by the water-line, and pulls the kayak towards her with a dangling foot, until Scoresby is within reach. Then she lets go with one hand to pass the sling under his belly. The puzzled beast lets her do what she wants on this strangest of days, and by the second or third attempt she's managed to untie the rope round her waist, pass it through the loop on the sling, and fashion a knot of sorts.

She pats his muzzle and calls up, 'He's hooked. Now haul him in.' Zannah watches the dog rise out of the kayak cockpit, looking around as if he does this every day. She climbs up the anchor chain, keeping close by, to offer reassurance, but soon sees he needs none. When Scoresby's dangling just below the rail she calls again: 'That's him!'

There's a pause, then Gideon's face appears over the rail, and the pain it bears is gone the moment he sees his dog, who responds by licking his face. With an effort Gideon lifts him over the rail and on to the deck. Scoresby cannot contain his delight once the sling is undone. He races round the deck, his tail pounding the bulwarks and hatch covers and twins as he tears by, searching every opening for a long-absent parrot. If his missing ship can suddenly return, then why not Pirate, his missing companion?

Zannah runs off to ring the bell again, and on her return asks, 'Where's Apollitacq?'

'Who?'

'You've been sharing a pigpen with a man whose name you don't know?'

'We weren't introduced.' Gideon's still affecting nonchalance. 'He went below.'

'You're sure there's no one else on board?'

Gideon nods.

'Then what's he doing?'

Gideon shrugs, but not out of nonchalance. He genuinely does not know.

Zannah drops down the companionway steps to the dim light of the hold. The wood underfoot is slippery with oil, and sticky with blood, and the whole place smells like a slaughterhouse. Large lumps of meat lie around, some with fins or flippers attached. Zannah gags. *These creatures rescued us. They sang foghorn hymns. Now look at them.*

There are stabbing and slurping noises somewhere behind her, as a bone knife cuts through flesh now dead. She scarcely dare turn around, especially when she hears the heavy breathing of the Aleut surgeon as he works. And when she does turn round and her eyes meet his, burning with urgent anger, she can hardly bear to look at what he is doing. His knife cuts, and pulls, and draws, and then is lain aside, as he delves into the bloody hunk with his bare hands, and then his arms, up the elbow. He looks at her as he works. 'Qamnuur!' he says. 'Qamnuur!'

His fevered activity suddenly stops, and a smile flickers across his face. He looks down, and pulls, slowly and steadily, as if he has hold of something precious. When his blood-smothered hands are visible at last Zannah sees between them a large round object the size of a man's head. Apollitacq treats it with reverence, looking around for a cloth to wipe the blood away and another to wrap it up in. He holds the cushioned bulk as delicately as he can, then lowers one ear to its mossy surface. He listens: and a smile as wide as the Bering Strait spreads across his anxious face. 'Qamnuur!' he says once more, and holds it out for her to listen too.

Zannah's not sure, but she thinks she can persuade herself there's a sound within; a scratching, perhaps, or a rolling-over. What strikes her more is the warmth of the mossy surface as it brushes her ear. She smiles back at him. 'Gumnor?' she ventures, not sure how to pronounce it. He nods vigorously, 'Qamnuur! Qamnuur!'

Together they climb the companionway to the deck, where the fog is thinning. Zannah sounds the bell again, and as she does so Apollitacq lowers the strange object on to a pile of furs in a corner of the pigpen, and covers it over with other furs lying about.

When he turns back it is to be confronted by Scoresby, growling already in guard of his ship. If

Apollitacq is surprised to see him there he hides it well, and in a moment Scoresby's allowing himself to be patted warmly before continuing his circuit of the deck.

Zannah turns to Gideon. 'What now?' she asks.

The little fleet of kayaks has closed up, to stay together in the fog, and all are listening hard as they round the headland that brings them into the bay. Fog-beasts are calling, in the deeper water to the north, while somewhere near the shore there tolls at intervals a distant mournful bell. 'That's my ship,' whispers Joshua, more to himself than anyone else, and not yet steering towards it. He listens harder, trying to gauge the distance, but it takes no effort to hear the awful shriek that takes the place of the next bell.

'And that's my daughter,' says Simva, instantly turning the kayak towards the source of the terrible cry.

'Wait!' hisses Joshua, digging his paddle in to slow her progress ahead of the fleet. 'Weapons ready . . . one in each kayak to paddle . . . we'll go slowly and quietly.'

Simva sees the sense in this and waits while he lays his paddle on the deck, and readies his rifle, adjusting the sights for close range. On either side Tukum and Kanaka prepare harpoons and throwing boards. The kayaks fan out, and wheel towards the shore in line abreast, each crew a duo of silent firm intent.

'We haul the kayak up,' says Gideon. 'And then the anchor.'

'What?' Zannah's amazed.

'Vincent's coming back to find the ship . . . reclaimed.'

'We can't sail her – just us – in this fog. It's madness.'

'Oh yes we can. There's an off-shore wind, nothing very strong. There are no other ships about, and, once we're past the reef, no obstacles to speak of.' He hauls himself to a standing position, braced against the fore mast. 'I will not leave her here for him. *I will not.* I'd rather sink her right now.'

She can tell he means it, and it will be useless to oppose him, so without a word she makes for the stern, and the bell, once again.

'Something not right,' grumbles Sven to Vincent in the next boat. 'The bell – not right. I could swear I heard a dog, then a scream.'

Vincent dismisses him. 'Your fearful ears unman you, Sven. I heard nothing.' But even he cannot dismiss the next sound the foggy air brings: the unmistakable creak of the *Unicorn*'s capstan, and the clank of her anchor chain as it is hauled in. Vincent is speechless for four or five heartbeats, then puts the rudder hard over to turn his gig around. He roars out to his boats and beyond, a disbelieving cry: 'Some villain steals my ship, men! Back! Back to the bell!'

His ship! Joshua wheels round, as Simva spins the kayak. Vincent's somewhere behind them. Tukum signals to spread out, and the kayaks disperse to watch, and listen, and wait, harpoons raised.

'We're not strong enough,' says Zannah, as she slumps against the capstan. 'The kayak was easy to raise, but this anchor . . .'

Gideon thumps himself for not thinking more clearly. 'Then we slip it. We mark it with a buoy on a rope, and just let it drop. We'll pick it up after . . . after whatever happens.'

Joshua's kayak bobs silently as he and Simva await

Vincent's oncoming boats; obscured still from view by the fog, but all too audible in their creaking oars, and Vincent's gruff orders to drive his breathless oarsmen on.

Simva senses, more than sees, the other kayaks on either side, while in front of her Joshua raises his rifle to his shoulder, and lowers his cheek to its damp wooden stock. 'Remember,' Simva whispers urgently, leaning forward as far as she can. 'He has hostages.'

Joshua nods, but doesn't look up from his sights. He waits, trying to relax his body, so as to absorb the movement of the kayak, and not transmit it to his gun. Behind him Simva struggles to suppress the turmoil within her. Nearby, to the left, Tukum and Attu are poised, water dripping from their raised harpoons; while, to the right, Hal and Kanaka tighten their grip on their unsheathed knives. No one breathes.

One shot, thinks Joshua. *Maybe two. Make them count. And if it's Vincent, he'll take both bullets.* A boat takes form from the fog, rowed hard by four men, its redundant sail furled up on the mast. Joshua swings his sights from the figures in the bows to the face of the steersman in the stern, desperate for it to be Vincent.

Sven's voice tells him it is not, and again, just as when the ship was first stolen, Joshua cannot bring himself to shoot a man he has sailed so far with. He lowers his aim, and fires twice into the bows of the boat, below the water-line.

Urgent shouts rise up all around, but, to Simva's relief, unmingled with the screams of wounded men. Sven's voice comes again. 'One man to bail, others all row,' and shots ring out from where he is sitting. Other guns sound on either side. There is a buzzing, as of bees, and then a fizz as a bullet hits the water close by. The paddle jumps in Simva's hands, kicking hard at her wrists. Splinters fly, and when next she looks down it is to see a neat round hole in her paddle.

'Back!' yells Joshua. 'We are outgunned!' As Simva paddles swiftly in reverse, Joshua lets off two more shots, but his aim is off amid the bucking of the kayak.

Sven's boat is already lower in the water, and slowing down, as its bilges fill, and more men quit rowing to bail. With Simva steadying the kayak, Joshua takes careful aim again, and fires once more into the hull of the sinking craft, to be quite sure it poses no more threat.

From away to the right come the sounds of a struggle – grunts, and yells, and splashes – but before Simva can sweep the kayak round, Hal's cry of victory rises above the conflict. 'We have the boat!' he shouts.

'And Vincent?' Joshua shouts back.

'Not here,' calls Kanaka.

Joshua and Simva peer about as the fog thins further. There is a distant yell in Aleut, and Simva wheels round 'There!' she shouts: and she is right. Rowing hard towards the shore, pursued by kayaks, is the largest of the *Unicorn*'s boats. Joshua slips his rifle under the deck straps, and joins Simva in her fast but fluent paddling. 'He's not getting away,' he says. 'Not this time.'

As the shots and shouts of conflict echo ahead of them, Gideon looks to Zannah, but only for a moment. They've unfurled just one sail – the main – and are now sheeting it in to catch the scanty wind; while on the wheel Apollitacq holds the ship's course while she gathers speed.

There's a ripple at her bow-wave now, and Gideon thrills to feel her movement underfoot. He's no idea where he is going, or what the next step is, but to be on board her again, and in motion too, is almost enough in itself. Despite his pain, and his fear, and his concern for his kin and his crewmen, he cannot help but smile.

Another, closer, shot rends the air somewhere off the port bow, followed by Vincent's unmistakable voice, urging his oarsmen on. Gideon scrambles to the stern as fast as his useless leg will let him. He crawls, and hops, and swings on the rigging, till he reaches the wheel, and takes it from Apollitacq.

When Zannah sees, to her dismay, that the ship is turning to steer directly towards noises in the fog, she dashes sternwards after her brother. She struggles to wrestle the wheel back round, but Gideon has jammed it tight, and his eyes flash at her, as he resists her efforts and entreaties. 'I'm going to run him down,' he spits, through teeth set tight. 'He'll steal no ships, nor men, nor fog-beasts again.'

Zannah continues her futile tug-of-war. 'But he's not alone!'

There's another shot, much closer now, and a bullet pings off the compass binnacle just in front of the helm. They both look up. Dead ahead, and freed now of fog, is Vincent's boat. His oarsmen ply their blades even more desperately, as they see the ship bear down upon them. Vincent holds the tiller hard over with one foot, and stands like a pendulum, swinging to fire in turn at the kayaks behind him and the ship now looming in front.

Gideon unjams the wheel long enough to wrench it round and match Vincent's turn, so the boat still lies dead ahead, as the vessels fast converge. Seeing this, the oarsmen drop their blades and scramble for the far gunwale. 'Draw on, you dogs, draw on!' rages Vincent. 'Or will I shoot you too?'

Before he has a chance his crew, to a man, leap into the sea, their limbs thrashing in desperate efforts to swim aside from the *Unicorn's* bows.

Still Vincent fires, standing now before the mast of his wallowing boat, to steady himself. He roars his defiance at the ship he stole, as if she is seeking revenge herself, pumping bullet after bullet into the rising mass of her bows, till his weapon is empty and he can only hurl it aside with an incoherent yell.

Gideon looks steadily ahead, arms locked round the spokes of the wheel. He will not meet his sister's pleading gaze.

'We've beaten him,' she says softly. 'Must he make us killers too?'

She has his eyes now: and she will not let him look away. She takes her hands from the wheel and lays them lightly on top of his, to tell him that whatever way the ship steers now, they'll steer her there together.

'A curse upon you all!' screams Vincent, as the *Unicorn* drives towards him. He closes his eyes to await the crushing of his boat below him, and the rush of icy water, but it does not come: and when he opens them again it is to see the ship heeled over as her bows swing away. The ship's side strikes the boat, to stove in the gunwale and throw Vincent off balance. He grips the mast as the boat scrapes down the vessel's side, and his fierce gaze sweeps the deck for the identity of these pirates. When he sees, at the helm, Gideon and Zannah embracing the wheel and each other, he is silenced, his curses and raging frozen by the awful truth.

Gideon comes to the rail. 'Eskimo spawn!' he shouts. 'Eskimo spawn did this!'

Vincent opens his mouth, but any reply is cut off in his throat, for there is a whoosh, and a squelching, splintering thunk, as Apollitacq hurls a heavy harpoon from the stern rail. It strikes Vincent full in the chest, and pins him to the mast. The shock of it spills down the sail behind him, and as Vincent writhes in silent agony, his feet tangle in the sail's ropes, and it fills with wind.

The boat veers off down wind, towards the thicker fog, pursued by the horrified stares of the kayakers, the crewmen splashing in the water, and the twins on the ship. None makes to follow him. Just before the fog swallows him up the twins see him spit blood. Vincent's voice, when it comes, is not a cry of pain, or even a moan against this ebbing of his life: it is an order.

'Rescue!' he demands. 'I am Noah Vincent!'

There is no reply but silence.

'Rescue me! I am The Crow! All my wealth to any man who will rescue me!'

Zannah rings the bell, long and loud, partly to drown out his cries, but mainly to alert all those in, or on the water, to the ship's position. Between them Apollitacq and Gideon haul the mainsail and the helmwheel round in opposite directions, to heave the ship to, and bring her to a halt. Zannah continues ringing the bell as ropes are lowered for boats and kayaks to make fast, and ladders for their sailors to clamber to the deck. She continues ringing the bell long after she's sure there is no one else on the water to hear it, and only stops when the deck is full of noise.

Most of the racket comes from Apollitacq and the other hostages, dancing a reel of reunion with their kin. Hal and Kanaka exchange victory whoops with Tukum and Attu, while Scoresby barks furiously at a shivering and silent Sven, and his sullen fearful crew-mates. Joshua doesn't join in, but walks in silence round and round the deck, running his hands over his battered but beloved vessel, as if to comfort her he'd never again let her out of his sight.

Gradually, one by one, they become aware of another noise, rising around them on all sides: a swelling foghorn chorus, as from an entire choir of fog-beasts, circling the ship in great numbers. The noise swells and soars and climbs in volume until it is impossible to speak and even Scoresby stops barking. The deck vibrates with the power of it. It grows louder again, till surely it can grow no louder, and then it comes to an abrupt and total stop, leaving echoes that bounce back from the shore, and last notes that resonate in the rope of the rigging.

It is then, in this ringing silence, that they hear again Vincent's voice, distant and dying, somewhere to the North.

'Rescue!' he's pleading now. 'I have wealth . . .'

Gideon turns to his sister. He runs one hand over the battered helmwheel of his rescued ship, and another over his wounded leg. 'No he doesn't,' he says. 'Not now.'

Zannah smiles back at him, and reaches in the bow of her kayak where it lies on the deck nearby. She holds out Gremykoff's blood-smeared telescope. 'He never did.'

CHAPTER 10
COMING HOME

'YOU MISSED SOME.' GIDEON POINTS WITH one of his new crutches at an oil-smeared plank in the *Unicorn*'s hold. Sven glares back at him. He's on hands and knees, in front of a tub of water and a scrubbing brush, and if his ankles were not manacled together, his look would spell death to anyone foolish enough to anger him. Gideon gazes unflinchingly back, tightens his grip on the crutch, and jabs it forward, as both pointer and threatened weapon. 'Just there.' Sven hisses Norwegian curses through gritted teeth, and picks up the brush again.

Elsewhere in the hold other men, unmanacled and unmuttering, work more willingly. Sven's erstwhile crew-mates were not complicit in stealing the ship, and Joshua has seen how they suffered under Vincent's rule.

He has no wish to outdo him, by way of punishment, and besides, the ship needs them.

High in the rigging, Zannah works alongside Simva and Jacques, checking sails, fastening buntlines, retying sheets and clews and tacks. She breaks off to take in the view of Oonalashka, laid out below. The *Unicorn* is one among a gaggle of ships that cluster in the bay, swinging at anchor in the wind – a southerly today. They bob in the light swell, dipping their bows, as if in salute, to the huddled town. Smoke from the Aleut houses streaks across the pebbled beach and half-mile crescent of water to the ships, ferrying the smells of cooking and craft. To the west, Mount Ballyhoo wears its early winter's mantle of snow with pride. Eagles soar black against the sun-sparkled white of the mountain's flanks. In the east, near the cemetery, a football match sends up shouts, in Aleut and English, ignored alike by the kayakers coming home from the sea. A contemplative eagle sits atop the church spire's Russian cross, roughly of a height with the ship's tallest mast. It seems to be staring back at her.

'A fine sight,' says Simva, from the yard arm to her right. Zannah nods, suddenly silenced by the thought she'll not see it again.

'Ah preefair zis.' Jacques indicates the newly bright

decks of the *Unicorn* below, where her two crews – the rightful and the pirate – have laboured long and hard to prepare her for departure. 'And to zink of whair she weel take us.'

Zannah glances down again. One of the many boats plying between the shore and the ships, is headed towards the *Unicorn*. She immediately recognises the tall bearded figure in the bows. 'Visitors!' she shouts to Joshua on deck. 'One of them's Gremykoff!' And she scrambles down the rigging, reaching deck just as Gideon, alerted by her call, hops up from the hold. They gather at the port quarter, where the boat ladder hangs: but it is Captain Healy, not the priest, who is first up.

He is followed by three fresh-faced strangers, who look the ship over with experienced eyes, and then two Oonalashka Aleut, and finally by Gremykoff, who hangs back by the stern to witness what comes next.

Joshua strides forward, with a hand outstretched for Healy. 'Welcome aboard my ship.' Gideon and Zannah both hear, in the way he says it, something of a challenge: as if Healy might bring with him some doubt in the matter.

'I see you have her again, as you warned you would.' Healy is terse and watchful.

'I do.' Joshua indicates his family and his crew, now

gathered on deck or hanging in the rigging above it. 'We do.'

'And the bloodshed?'

'Several men wetted, and frozen and frightened. But none badly injured or killed – save that villain Vincent.' Joshua almost spits out his name.

'At whose hand?' Healy runs his eyes over the crew. 'Murder is murder, however foul the victim.' Zannah feels his stare bore into Hal, to her left, then skip over her to settle on Nathan. 'At whose hand, I say?'

'Mine.' Zannah's voice is hesitant, but clear and firm. Her right hand is raised. Her left takes Gideon's crutch, as he raises his own right hand: 'And mine.'

'Mine too.' Nathan says, switching his paint brush to his left hand, and raising his right. 'And me.' Rosa emerges from the deck house, her hand already raised. Hal raises his left hand. 'Mine as well.' Jacques calls down from the rigging: 'Moi aussi,' followed closely by Kanaka, in Polynesian, and Simva in Aleut.

Finally, after a pause while Healy takes in this unanimous confession, Joshua raises his right hand, the same hand he's extended in greeting moments before. 'Ignore them,' he says. 'This hand is a captain's hand, and a captain is responsible for what his crew do. A shipless captain, when Vincent met his end, I grant you, but a captain nonetheless. So if you come here as the law, to throw any hand in irons, let it be mine, and mine alone, and let it be now.'

He extends his wrists to Healy, who holds him long in a fathomless gaze from deep-set dark eyes. A smile stirs the fringes of his beard. 'Be at ease, Captain Murphy. Vincent will prey no more upon ships, and their crews and the Aleut. There is justice in this, even if your justice is achieved by . . . unconventional means. You may leave unhindered.' Tension eases all around the deck, and Gideon and Zannah exchange quick glances of relief.

Healy's not done, though. He turns to the young men he's brought aboard. 'And to aid in your passage south I bring crewmen, if you will have them. John Quarrie, Lon Boofus, Waldo McFee. Neither they nor I wish to have them clutter up this port through an Alaskan winter, and teaching native children to beat us at your English sports. They are seamen, or so they tell me. I will trade them for the Americans you found in Vincent's company.'

Joshua eyes the young men, who know how to weigh up a ship, and most masters, but not a captain or a crew like this. 'Sailors, eh?' he asks them.

'Aye, sir,' replies the one called Waldo.

'Cape Horn men?'

Waldo steps forward to show the gold ring in his left ear, the ear nearest land when rounding the notorious Cape. Joshua nods approval. Lon Boofus grins, and shows his other ear. 'Went round the wrong way,' he mumbles.

There's a pause before John Quarrie speaks. 'My ears ain't big enough for all *my* roundings. Both ways.'

'But I need only two sailors: I have not room nor food for more.' Gideon meets Zannah's eye: both know this is not true.

'It's a test,' whispers Zannah. Gideon nods.

The three young men step aside, without hesitation. Lon Boofus speaks for them all. 'Then we will find another ship, captain. For when we sail we sail together.'

Joshua smiles for the first time since Healy came aboard. 'You answer well, and you are welcome, all three, for this vessel sails the same way.' He extends his smile to his twins, who return it redoubled. 'But it's a warmer place we go to than the Horn.' He shakes their hands, one by one, and there's a general clamour of greetings, and introductions, broken only by an angry clanking of chains.

'And what of me?' demands Sven, from the steps to

the hold. 'I am put to work as a slave in chains, and taunted by half-native cripples.'

Healy's waited for this. 'Ah, Mister Ahlborg. I have asked of all the ships in harbour: but none will have you, for they know of your mutinous nature.' He lets this sink in. 'I will free you, and take you ashore, there to spend the winter.'

'To do what?' asks Sven, indignantly. He doesn't notice Simva's almost envious glance.

'To tend my church.' Gremykoff speaks at last, his voice booming out as if in a sermon. 'Where, as you work, you will seek forgiveness, every day, for your crimes.'

Sven is stunned by this news, and can find nothing to say, even when Nathan tosses him the key to his ankle chains. He follows Healy, as he makes for the boat, walking the gauntlet of accusing silence from the shipmates he has betrayed: from Nathan with whom he's sailed every ocean of the world; from Rosa, who has cooked him thousands of meals; from Joshua, who has trusted him with his ship and his life; from Simva, who has trusted him with her children, and, fiercest of all, from the twins themselves.

'I never liked him,' says Hal, when Sven has gone. 'Couldn't stand him talking all the time.'

'You've 'ad it with old Waldo 'ere, then,' says

John Quarrie. 'Nothing shuts 'im up. Only time 'is mouth's not full o' talk is when it's full o' food.'

Gideon listens in to the developing banter: it's already promising to be a good trip.

'Do you trust him in your church?' Joshua asks Gremykoff.

'There is little to steal, and no way to sell it. And humble work will be good for his soul.' He peers down into the hold. 'A lesson I see you've already applied. What did you do with the – the *remains?*'

'We saved one barrel of oil for you. The Aleut would not use it themselves, but agreed it might light your church.'

Gremykoff nods. 'And make Sven's penance even more apt. He must fill the church lamps with oil from the sacred beast he hunted in the hope it would bring him wealth. How fitting. And the rest?'

'A pyre,' Zannah breaks in. 'Like the Vikings. We floated the pieces of carcass on a plank, and soaked it in oil, and set fire to it. We watched it for miles as we sailed here. It lit up the underneath of the clouds like a . . .'

'Like a sunset.' It's Gideon's turn to interrupt.

Joshua and Simva catch each other's eye. They've just heard something they weren't aware they'd missed. Joshua smiles: but the sadness of pending departure weighs too heavily to let Simva return it.

'A sunset in the North.'

'And it didn't go out.'

'It might be burning now.'

After the farewells, the *Unicorn*'s anchor is lifted and she slips through the motley fleet gathered in the bay. Joshua's pride in helming her is undiminished by her battered scruffiness and evident to all the scowling sailors who spat at his kayak.

Nathan and Hal stand at the bow, with pistols tucked into their belts, lest any promyshleniki seek vengeance for Vincent.

'We shall not need these,' says Nathan. 'He was the kind who never have friends.'

Hal peers astern. Gremykoff's boat, with a now unmanacled Sven has just reached the shore. He nods. 'Just enemies and fellow-travellers. None will weep for him.'

Zannah and Gideon stand side by side at the starboard rail, as ship after ship decked with surly Russian fur-traders and hard-eyed American gold-diggers slips astern. 'Smile at them,' he says, grinning broadly. 'They hate it when you do that.'

Zannah notes that it is true: the warmer and wider her brother's smile, the colder and harder the returning stares. But she doesn't feel much like smiling herself.

Once out of the bay Joshua hands the helm over to a delighted Tukum, who has never steered anything larger than a kayak. He steps forward to the twins, and stands behind them as they approach the Priest Rock, the marker of the exit from the bay and arrival at the open sea. Behind and above it the mountains soar sheer from the sea, sparkling white in the early winter sun.

Zannah looks up at her father. There's no masking the sadness in her eyes or in her voice. 'Will we ever see it again?'

Joshua lays a hand on her shoulder. 'Yes, Zannah. We will.'

'When?'

Joshua looks along the rail to where Simva stands apart, with only Scoresby for company. She lifts her head and lowers her hood, the better to feel the chill wind that is to take her away from this landscape she loves. 'Sooner than you think,' he says, softly.

Zannah frowns, but Joshua pre-empts her question. 'You didn't notice, did you?'

'Notice what?'

'I did. Your mother too. Something you've not done for a very long time.'

Now Gideon's frowning too: but Joshua continues. 'When you were talking to Gremykoff, about the pyre. Remember how you described it?'

Zannah does. 'It lit up the clouds –'

'– like a sunset.' Gideon finishes for her, and suddenly both of them realise he's right. It's been most of a year since either finished the other's sentence. But neither noticed that it had stopped, or has now begun again.

Joshua turns to Simva, but her eyes are closed as she lets the wind tug her hair and raises her face to the chilly sun. When he speaks, it is clearly to her, but his voice is so soft only his twins can hear. 'Seeing you two, and hearing the words you say, come together again, has set me thinking. I may have learnt something from you. When my ship and I were parted I had no thought but of her recovery: now that I have her back, I see there is much I have missed.' And he steps forward, and wraps an arm round his wife's startled shoulders.

'A more controlled arrival than last time, eh?' says Hal at the helm, to Gideon, on the other side of the wheel, as the *Unicorn* slips gently into Barbera Bay. Gideon recalls – has never forgotten – the fight with the bucking, spinning wheel as the ship drove up the beach on that stormy night, a lifetime ago.

He looks ahead to where a fleet of kayaks has already put out from the shore to greet them. 'And a warmer welcome, too.'

Even before the anchor is dropped there are kayaks clustered at the base of the boarding ladder, and Aleut keen to come aboard. Apollitacq is among them, though less eager than some to reboard the ship where he and his fellow hostages suffered so long under Vincent. He lets Attu, and Amaq, his wife, climb the ladder before him, but gets a less gruff greeting than they do from Scoresby as he reaches the deck. He pats the dog's head and points him out to Amaq, with words that generate laughter.

'He says Scoresby's a new kind of animal,' Zannah translates for Waldo. 'A dog that travels by kayak.'

Apollitacq turns next to the twins, and pulls them towards him, laying a hand on each shoulder. He presents them proudly to his wife, as his rescuers, who had freed him, and defeated Vincent. Amaq drops to one knee, and rubs noses with each of them, unembarrassed by the tears which flow over her broad cheeks.

Gremykoff looks on benignly, and when Amaq dries her eyes enough to see him, she snaps to her feet and kisses his outstretched hand, anxiety on her face. Gremykoff speaks too fast for Zannah to follow, but his words, and his gestures towards the twins, the crew, and Joshua, together with Amaq's huge relief, all tell the story well enough. Her husband is to face no consequences from Healy or anybody else for launching his harpoon at Vincent's heart.

Lon Boofus has missed all this. He stands in the bows with Simva, staring at the shore. 'But where did you live?' he asks, seeing nothing but low bumps in the hillside, covered with grass and unmarked by any cooking smoke now that the barbera is empty again.

'I would show you,' Simva replies, 'but I do not wish to revisit my home now that I have left it.'

'But surely this ship is your home?'

'We are lucky,' Joshua breaks in. 'For we now have two homes.' He looks at Simva, and pats the beams of his beloved vessel. 'This ship is made of wood, and can travel the world: but wood comes from trees, which need roots, and soil in which to grow.' He fixes his gaze on his twins. 'So it is with people.' And now it is Simva he holds in his eyes.

'We sail to the islands of the south, where we will

travel, and trade, as before.' He turns to Gremykoff and raises his voice for all to hear. 'But look for us at the spring equinox, when we will return to this bay, to summer with you, next and every summer, if we may.'

Zannah's heart leaps, and she looks to her smiling mother. As they take it in, Gremykoff relays the news to the Aleut, who react with smiles, and nodding heads. Tukum steps up beside the priest, and whispers in his ear. Gremykoff nods, and Tukum addresses the twins, their parents, and the crew, slowly and deliberately, holding each in his dark eyes as he pauses for Gremykoff to translate.

'Siberians came, and took our sea-cows, till none remain. Russians came, and took our otters, leaving us few. Americans and English came, and took our whales, and our salmon, till our seas and our rivers have emptied.'

He looks at Joshua. 'When you came we feared what you would take. But when Vincent returned to hunt our sacred fog-beasts, you fought alongside us, so now they are safe.' He smiles at the twins. 'You are always welcome here, and we will tend your barbera till equinox comes.' He gives a bow, and his kinsmen cheer.

Unnoticed amid all this talking, Apollitacq has been busy, tracing a thin blood-red line around the ship, just under the rail, from one bow, across the stern, and back to the bow. He has almost finished when he calls the twins over, and hands them a seal-hair brush each.

'It's a spirit line,' says Zannah, to a hesitant Gideon. 'Like they paint inside their kayaks. It marks the soul of the ship.'

Apollitacq lowers his bowl of paint to the deck, and bids them finish his handiwork. Zannah takes the starboard bow, and Gideon port, and slowly, carefully they trace the finger-wide line forward, till they meet at the very stem of their regained ship, and the spirit line is joined, to enclose her deck and make her whole again.

Somewhere in the distance a foghorn sounds. The new hands look about with puzzled glances, but meet only shrugs. Zannah and Gideon lower their brushes and return the paint to Apollitacq. Their smiles broaden with each foghorn call. For as yet only they know that each call creates a stirring within a rescued egg, securely wrapped in warm furs, below deck. And the stirring is stronger, every time the fog-call comes.